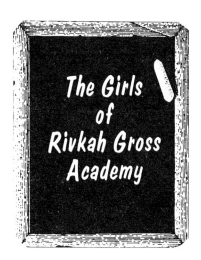

The Girls
of
Rivkah Gross
Academy

THE
SILENT
SUMMER

Sukey Gross

CIS
P·U·B·L·I·S·H·E·R·S
New York · London · Jerusalem

A CIS PUBLICATION

Distributed in the U.S., Canada and overseas by
C.I.S. Publishers and Distributors
180 Park Avenue, Lakewood, New Jersey 08701
(201) 905-3000 Fax: (201) 367-6666

Distributed in Israel by
C.I.S. International (Israel)
Har Nof, Jerusalem
Tel: 02-538-935

Distributed in the U.K. and Europe by
C.I.S. International (U.K.)
1 Palm Court, Queen Elizabeth Walk
London, England N16
Tel: 01-809-3723

Book and Cover Design by Ronda Kruger Israel
Cover and Illustrations by Hedy Shiman
Typography by Chaya Hoberman

Printed by Gross Brothers, Inc., Union City, New Jersey

The mother concentrates all her love
In the child she forms and develops
Fusing all her energy to mold
Neshamos emanating *midos tovos.*

The father awakens in the early dawn
Davens, of Hashem's name always aware
Spends every spare moment learning Torah and
Teaching his children to care.

My parents and in-laws have striven
To guide and to illuminate
With appreciation to Hashem I recognize
their struggles
In their memory and יבדלו לחיים in their honor,
this series I do dedicate.

לז״נ אבי מורי
ר׳ משה מרדכי ז״ל בן ר׳ חיים צבי סטבסקי נ״י

לז״נ חמתי
רבקה גראס ע״ה בת ר׳ אברהם

לז״נ דודתי
שולמית פריידל עטקין ע״ה בת ר׳ חיים צבי סטבסקי נ״י

ת.נ.צ.ב.ה.

In honor of my esteemed mother Mrs. Chana Rubin.
In honor of my distinguished father-in-law Rabbi Moshe Gross.
With great honor, respect and in appreciation to my husband
Rabbi Meir Gross.
A thank you to the initial reviewers, Layah, Shayndy, Malkie,
Mordechai, Bayla, Avrami, Avigayil and Michal.
Special thanks to Dr. Elliot Goldberg and Mrs. Naomi Landesman.

Table of Contents

🍀 **1** 🍀

GOALS FOR THE SUMMER

"**M**y diamonds!" the old lady cried. "You're trampling on my diamonds!"

Sara and I were standing near the old country road that ran through Camp Rivkah, the camp affiliated with Rivkah Gross Academy. We were AJCs, Assistant Junior Counselors, and we were in the middle of a counselors' hunt. The staff members had all hidden in secret places throughout the camp grounds, and it was the job of the campers to find and capture them.

Sara and I had just been found, but since we were only simple AJCs, lowest in the hierarchy of the camp, it was not surprising that the girls who had just captured us had abandoned us almost immediately; the girls thought they had seen Ruchie, the head counselor, hiding in the distance and had run off to capture bigger game.

Having been "captured," we were expected to return to the main house by ourselves, but instead, we found ourselves engrossed in the bizarre scene that unfolded in front of us. Sara and I stood in place, under the trees and hidden from sight, watching the old lady in puzzled fascination.

The old lady was dressed in outlandish clothing. She wore a long, heavy black skirt and three heavy sweaters, one on top of the other. Covering the front of her outfit was a faded flowered apron, now muddy, stained and ragged. She wore a large straw hat with a discolored red flower drooping solemnly from a stained headband. The gray woolen gloves on her hands had unraveled at the fingertips. Tears streaked her dusty face. She seemed a pitiful soul as she concentrated on patting the ground, while she continued to mutter comments about diamonds and *chessed*, oblivious to the happy cries of the campers and their activities.

And what was this about diamonds?

"What's going on?" I asked Sara. "Who is that old lady and why is she screaming about diamonds?"

Sara shrugged.

"I really don't understand what is happening here," Sara answered. "That lady is Tante. We used to think she was a real sweet elderly woman. I don't know why she is saying these strange things. I doubt very highly that she has any diamonds hidden in her garden."

"But look at her," I insisted. "She's bending down on the ground and patting those little mounds of dirt. She's actually crying."

Sara shrugged again.

"What is she doing in the camp?" I asked Sara.

It was only the second day of camp, and I hadn't really been introduced to every little detail about Camp Rivkah.

"It seems she was a very close friend of the founders of the camp," Sara explained. "She had helped them many times throughout their lives, both monetarily and through acts of kindness. Because she didn't have any family, she would always come up to the camp during the summer months and help open and close the camp. From what I understand, she used to manage the kitchen. When the original founders died, about ten years ago, she still kept coming to camp, but she has just been living in her little cottage. Nobody ever bothers her, and she always greets everyone with a happy smile. She is a harmless and an extremely thoughtful person. I wonder . . ."

"What do you wonder?" I said with a sigh.

Sara Goodman's curiosity has always led us into very unusual predicaments. She's a perky individual with blonde hair and freckles on her nose. She lives for adventure, mystery and excitement.

I am just the opposite. My name is Bracha Friedman. I am short (I like to describe myself as petite) with a long, dark brown ponytail. My best feature is my nose. It's a perfect nose, a little turned up at the tip. My personality, however, is the exact opposite of Sara's. Every adventure she is ready to jump into, I have to first test out with my big toe. Being best friends with Sara, though, doesn't give me much of a chance to get used to the water before I'm abruptly pulled in.

"I wonder . . ." Sara thoughtfully repeated. "Maybe Tante really does have diamonds buried in her garden."

"And what do you propose to do about finding out?" I asked Sara impatiently and perhaps a little sarcastically.

I could imagine what Sara was planning to do, and as my cautious stomach was warning me with its butterflies, I was in for an unusual time.

"We will meet here after *lailah tov* and see what we can discover." Sara stated her decision strongly and with determination.

"If you are thinking of digging up the garden," I answered hesitantly, "wouldn't that mean destroying someone else's property?"

"Oh, don't worry so much," Sara answered flippantly as she began to walk away in the direction of the main building. "The camp owns all the property, even Tante's cottage and garden. There's no problem. We're allowed access to all camp grounds."

I followed Sara, not entirely convinced. Sara would never do anything against *Halachah*, I argued with myself in my mind, so it must be all right to go in Tante's garden without first asking for permission. After all, I reassured myself, hadn't the campers nonchalantly run through the garden in their quest for staff members during the counselors' hunt?

I shrugged my shoulders.

"Hey, wait for me!" I called out to Sara.

She turned around and paused, allowing me the extra moment to catch up. I was surprised when I saw the look on her face. The impulsive Sara was a picture of study and thoughtfulness.

"You might be right," Sara said. "I see a dilapidated picket fence around the little garden. Maybe it was put there to give Tante a little more privacy. Perhaps we really aren't permitted to venture into her garden."

I was glad Sara had finally agreed with me. It seemed too good to be true.

"Does that mean you have changed our plans for tonight?" I asked.

Sara shook her head in the negative.

"Of course not," she answered. "Maybe we won't dig up the garden. But there is definitely something unusual going on with Tante, and you and I distinctly heard her say the girls were trampling her diamonds. I still want to investigate. Come on and hurry now. It looks like the hunt is over. I really don't care which *ohel* won, but I can't wait for the ices they serve all the staff members after the hunt."

We both laughed and ran to the front of the main building. All the campers were lined up according to bunks, and we joined the rest of the AJCs on our line. Of course, since we were no longer campers but not quite staff members, we didn't stand in too perfect a straight line. We were too sophisticated to be bothered with the daily camp routine. Besides which, we were just interested in exchanging stories about our hiding places.

"Naomi," I called laughingly when I saw one of my friends from school dressed up in a masculine jacket and hat. "Are you rehearsing for a play?"

"No," Naomi laughed back, pulling the hat off of her head and allowing her light brown curls to cascade down her back. "Boy, that hat was really hot."

"Why were you wearing it?" Sara inquired.

"Well," Naomi answered. "Do you see that picnic table and bench in the corner?"

We all nodded.

"I dressed up in this jacket and hat," Naomi explained, "put a *sefer* in front of me and pretended I was one of the men sitting and learning."

We all laughed as we pictured the tall gangly Naomi playing the part of one of the local on-campus rabbis.

"Well, did it work?" Sara asked anxiously. I knew she was storing this little trick in her memory bank so she could use it to her benefit at some later date.

"It worked for about fifteen minutes," Naomi answered. "That is, until little Zevy came running across the lawn screaming, 'Tatty! Tatty!' He was followed by a bunch of kids from *Ohel Alef.* When they came up to me, Zevy started to cry, 'You're not my Tatty!' Then *Ohel Alef* captured me and brought me in."

"It was certainly a good idea," Sara said.

"Yes, Naomi," I added. "You definitely get points for originality."

At that moment, our counselor Binny handed us our ices. We lounged on the grass as the sky darkened and the deepening dusk enveloped us in its closeness. The ices were cool, and we smacked our lips appreciatively, savoring the sticky sweetness.

As the evening unfolded into the night, the younger campers retreated into their bunks to prepare for *lailah tov*. We lounged around talking among ourselves, entrusting secrets that only the covering darkness permitted us to divulge.

"Do you know, girls?" Binny began to confess. "I almost didn't come to camp this summer."

Since I was new to Camp Rivkah, I had only a slight idea as to what we would have missed if Binny would have opted to stay home that summer. But the girls who had been in the camp before began to vehemently protest.

"But, Binny!"

"You're the best!"

"What would Camp Rivkah be like without you?"

"You wouldn't dare not come!"

"Well, I almost didn't come to camp this year," Binny repeated. "I'm sure you know I am going to Seminary in Eretz Yisrael next year, *b'ezras Hashem.*"

We all nodded our heads. Most of the counselors would either be going to Eretz Yisrael in September or had just come back from Seminary in Eretz Yisrael in June.

Binny hesitated. I guess she was trying to explain herself without divulging too many family secrets.

"When I mentioned to my mother I wished to stay home this summer, she wouldn't let me," she said.

Of course, we all knew that Binny was here in camp, but we still sighed with relief that her mother had forced her to go to camp.

"I allowed my mother to convince me to come to camp," Binny continued, "if she would also get my eight-year-old cousin Aviva into camp."

As Binny hesitated again, we eyed one another, questioning without verbalizing.

Binny sat on the grass, surrounded by her fifteen devoted listeners. Her knees were bent up to meet her chin, and her arms were clasped around her knees, hugging them.

"Do you see?" Binny began again. "I brought my little cousin Aviva to camp in the hope that a camp environment could save her."

Binny stopped talking for a moment, and nobody uttered a sound in response. We could hear the chirping of the crickets and the soft rustling of the summer breeze in the trees.

"Aviva can't talk, you see, " she said. "Oh, she was a normal baby. She cried when it was appropriate. She was always laughing and even singing. She said Mama and then Dada at the right ages. She would babble constantly. Her mother, who is my aunt, would always have her perform and show off in front of the family. And you should have seen her with her dolls! In Aviva's eyes, those stuffed dolls and animals were real people. The imaginative games she would play with them . . ."

Binny's voice trailed off as she remembered the happier times in her cousin's household.

We wanted to question why Aviva couldn't talk, but we hesitated to pry. We should not have feared. Binny was going to tell us the whole sad story.

"Let me give you some background," she continued. "My mother and Aviva's father are sister and brother. They are about ten years apart in age. My uncle was born some years before the War and my mother a couple of years after. They were both born in America, but my aunt, my uncle's wife, was not.

"My Aunt Goldie had gone through the concentration camps. That's a story within itself, and I could tell you of many horrible and miraculous incidents that happened to her. Perhaps another time.

"Anyhow, my aunt and uncle didn't have any children. They had been married for about twenty years when the miracle occurred. When my Aunt Goldie was in her forties, little Aviva was born.

"You can't imagine the *simchah* in the household when Aviva was born. It was such an obvious *ness* that even the irreligious doctors proclaimed Aviva a miracle baby.

"She was the most beautiful baby. And so cherished and loved. You'll see her tomorrow, and you will see I am telling the truth. That's the tragedy of this whole affair. If you look at Aviva, she seems to be an absolutely normal child. There isn't any anger or hostility. The only sad thing is that she doesn't talk. Oh, up until she was about four, she was normal, maybe even above normal. But slowly, she stopped talking to her friends and even her mother. For a while, she would still sing in front of the family. But soon she stopped even that. Now, the only time you can hear her voice is when she is playing with her dolls. If she knows you are observing her, however, she just clams up.

"As you can well imagine, my aunt and uncle took Aviva from doctor to doctor. They spent thousands of dollars on the most respected specialists. No doctor could find a thing wrong with Aviva. And yet they could not give a concrete or definite reason why she doesn't talk.

"Oh, there are plenty of theories. One doctor suggested that the trauma of my aunt's years in the concentration camp had manifested itself as a hysterical reaction in her daughter. Another doctor felt it might have something to do with her having been born when my aunt was older. A third doctor said that maybe the family smothered Aviva with too much love and demanded too much from her by showing her off and that this had caused Aviva to protest to the point where she refused to speak at all."

Binny shrugged, as we silently scoffed at all these theories.

"Who knows? I felt, though, that perhaps if Aviva were in a different environment, surrounded by girls who are always laughing and playing, she would emerge from her silence. I told my mother I would come to camp only if I would be able to try.

"That's where you girls come in," Binny concluded. "I have a plan, and I need your help. How does a little child learn to talk? She is constantly exposed to words and learns the value of expression. I want all of you to think of different ideas to use when you work with Aviva."

"Work with Aviva?" Sara repeated.

"Yes," Binny nodded. "The AJCs this summer have a special job to do. You are all to be Aviva's big sisters. You'll divide into teams and work with her in different ways. Perhaps with our efforts, we can help bring about the miracle of reteaching Aviva to speak."

We all sat silently, concentrating on the task before us, thinking of different and unusual ideas to use while working with Aviva.

"Are we a team?" Binny asked us confidently, already knowing our response.

We all nodded our heads in the darkness, barely discerning the expression on Binny's face. And as the stars twinkled their approval, sixteen young hands were solemnly clasped together in anticipation of success.

❦ **2** ❦

NIGHT MANUEVERS

"**S**hhh," Sara whispered. "I don't want Binny or any of the other kids to follow us."

I was really trying to be quiet. But how do you tell your teeth to stop chattering?

It was way after *lailah tov*. Sara had decided that we should wait until everyone in the bunk was asleep before we ventured out to explore. Unfortunately, it wasn't until after midnight when everyone had quieted down.

After we had returned to our bunk, we had been very busy suggesting different ideas which could possibly help Aviva speak. Some girls suggested playing word games with her. Other girls thought it would be a good idea to tell her lots of stories. Sara and I hadn't really joined the discussion. I think we were too concerned about the next few hours to concentrate on looking for a cure for Aviva.

The moon was high in the sky. I was glad. All the familiar daytime shapes wore strange cloaks in the darkness. I imagined many different animals and unusual beings lurking in the deep shadows.

"Don't walk so fast," I whispered to Sara.

"What's the matter, Bracha?" Sara teased. "Are you afraid?"

Sara and I had gone through too many experiences together for me to pretend.

"Yes," I answered meekly. "But I'm coming with you anyhow. So please slow down."

Sara slowed her pace and even held my hand for good measure.

I saw the shape of Tante's cottage looming ahead in the darkness. I wondered what Sara planned to do when we arrived at the cottage. She hadn't expressed any further thoughts on the matter. There hadn't been much of a chance for us to talk privately.

Although it was a warm evening, I was glad I had decided to wear a sweatshirt over my heavy velour bathrobe. I tightened the hood and thrust my hands into the pockets. Was I really cold or was I just frightened?

We stopped beneath the trees at approximately the same spot from where we had observed Tante earlier that evening. Everything was quiet and dark. Tante's car was parked near the road where we were standing. The breeze stirred the leaves on the trees, and the night sounds were comforting even in their strangeness.

"What are we going to do now?" I questioned Sara.

"I really don't know," Sara replied with a shrug. "Origi-nally, I had planned to dig around the place where Tante had been patting the earth and mumbling those strange things. But now I think we would be messing around on private property, and it wouldn't be right."

"So?" I questioned further. I knew Sara had something up her sleeve.

"Well, first things first," she answered. "When we were here this evening, the car wasn't parked in that spot, was it?"

"No," I answered. "So what? Maybe Tante went shopping."

Sara placed her hand on the engine of the car. It was still warm to the touch. Obviously, the car had been used recently.

"At twelve o'clock at night?" she questioned.

"Maybe an all-night supermarket," I feebly suggested.

"It's not likely." Sara brushed off my suggestion in her typical manner.

"What was that?" I asked, frightened.

At first, I wasn't sure if I had actually heard something, or if I was letting my imagination play tricks on me.

Sara had also heard the noise. Her cold hands clutched my shaking ones.

"Shhh," she said. "There it is again."

It sounded like a moan. Or it might have been a groan. I seemed to hear somebody gasping for breath. It sounded like someone in pain. Or was it just my imagination giving undue importance to an innocent night sound of the country?

I tried to discern the direction from which the noise was coming. The bungalow was completely dark, and all the shades were drawn.

I looked at Sara and was surprised to see her laughing and pointing to the garden patch. Sitting right in the middle of Tante's garden patch, not far from the spot where she had been digging that evening, was a small gray bunny rabbit holding some lettuce in his paws and munching hungrily at his midnight snack. We both smiled, momentarily amused and distracted.

Suddenly, the bunny stopped eating and froze in position, and our smiles followed suit. This time, there was no mistake. All three of us had heard the same thing. And there was no denying the nature of those eerie sounds or from where they had originated. Coming from the open window of Tante's cottage, we could distinctly hear the sounds of moaning. It was definitely a cry of someone in pain.

The bunny rabbit dropped the food he was eating and quickly hopped off to his forest home. Sara and I exchanged frightened looks. Then we, too, quickly and silently followed suit.

❀ **3** ❀

A PERFECT PLAN

"**W**ake up, you sleepy head!"

I just turned over and ignored the noises.

"Come on," I vaguely heard from the distance. "This is your last chance."

I pulled the covers over my head and cuddled deep into my warm cocoon. It was bad enough that my face had been exposed to the cool morning air seeping in from the outside. I wasn't going to let the icy fingers of dawn invade the rest of my body.

In the distance, I heard some strange sounds. As I was trying to decipher the whispers, I heard a hushed count of "One, two, three." All of a sudden, I felt my covers pulled completely off of my body.

Standing around my bed, it looked like a mob had come to attack. And poised over me was my best friend Sara, holding a large *neigel vasser* cup of what I could only imagine to be ice-cold water.

The cup seemed to grow in size as I watched Sara begin to tip it over in slow motion right above my head. Instinct quickly took over. With a savage cry of attack, instead of rolling away, I deliberately aimed my bedroll at Sara's knees. She fell over onto Naomi's bed, reaching out at a number of girls to gain her balance. They were also caught off guard.

As the seven of us untangled ourselves laughingly from the floor and Naomi's bed, Sara picked up the cup she had planned on emptying over my head.

"Look, Bracha," she said, acting terribly insulted. "There was nothing in the cup. I wouldn't have been so cruel as to pour ice-cold water on your face so early in the morning."

I looked back at Sara sheepishly.

"Had I known that," I said, "I wouldn't have tackled you."

"Don't let her make you feel too guilty," Binny said as she came up from behind the crowd. "Sara had really wanted to use some cold water on you. I just told her that if she did she would be docked from swimming for the next couple of days. You know, *midah keneged midah*. Water," Binny pointed to the cup Sara was holding, "and water." She then proceeded to dramatize a swimming stroke.

Everyone laughed with cheerful abandon as we began

to truly awaken and prepare for *Shacharis*.

I sat down on my bed with my right foot on the mattress and completed tying my shoelaces.

"Psst," Sara whispered, leaning over the top of the bunk bed so that her freckled face was upside-down. "We've got to make some plans for today."

I looked at Sara and felt the urge to twist upside-down myself. Looking at her face in such an unusual position made me dizzy.

I knew the direction to which her mind was bent. I was also trying to think of some excuse to dig in Tante's garden. I also wanted to find out the source of the moans and groans.

Sara flipped down off of the top bunk bed and landed a little lopsidedly on Naomi's single bed next to mine.

"Got to practice that better," she whispered to herself as she rubbed her right hip.

"Be careful you don't hurt yourself," I said.

Sara shrugged it off. She was thinking about Tante's garden.

"Think up some plan," Sara commanded.

"I have been thinking," I replied hesitantly.

I used to be very nervous about venturing forth with my opinion. But being such a close friend of Sara's obviously rubbed off on me. Now I found myself only hesitating slightly when I had suggestions to make.

We began walking together to the *Shul* where all the middle and older bunks *davened* together.

"Didn't Binny say that the AJCs are to devote ourselves to *chessed* this summer?" I began.

"Yes," Sara answered patiently. Patience was not one of Sara's best virtues, but I guess she felt she had no choice but to be patient since she hadn't come up with an idea of her own.

"Well, we saw the younger bunks destroying Tante's garden," I continued. "Wouldn't it be an act of *chessed* to restore her garden to its proper condition?"

Sara jumped at the idea and literally began to skip and dance all the way to *davening*.

"Oh, yes," she sang. "And then we can investigate the cries of pain and at the same time search for the diamonds."

She slapped me on the back in her enthusiasm and nearly made me fall.

"Perfect," she said. "Perfect, in its simplicity!"

After *Shacharis*, we went to look at the activity chart. Girls from different bunks were shoving and pushing to see the chart which Ilana, the program director, had just posted. Everyone was waiting anxiously to find out the plans for the day.

"Okay," said Binny as she stepped away from the activity chart. "These are our activities. Our first two activities are *chessed*. After lunch, we have swimming, *machanayim* and computers."

Binny's announcement was greeted with loud cheers. All the activities planned for us for this day were fun activities.

Sara nudged me, and I nudged her back.

"Uh, Binny," Sara began.

"I'm glad you two are here together," Binny interrupted

before Sara was able to divulge our plan.

She began to walk more slowly, so within a few minutes we were behind the other AJCs.

"I need your help," Binny's voice lowered to a whisper. "All the girls have various suggestions for helping Aviva learn how to talk."

It took our brains a minute to shift gear. We had been so busy thinking of different ways and means to solve our mystery at the cottage that we had forgotten Binny's little cousin Aviva.

"I'm afraid, though," Binny continued, "that although the other girls sincerely wish to help, they might come on a little too strong."

I exchanged glances with Sara. Binny was too busy with her own thoughts to notice.

"Sara," she said. "You come from a large family, *bli ayin hora*. There must be millions of problems your sisters and brothers have encountered over the years. You know how to handle little children without looking down at them.

"And you, Bracha," Binny went on. "Although I don't know you that well, I have seen how sensitive you are to other people's feelings."

I began to blush, a problem I still haven't been able to overcome.

"I would like the two of you," she concluded, "to be the first to work with Aviva."

She made this statement without expecting us to protest. Sara and I exchanged glances once again. This time Binny did notice.

"Is there a problem?" she asked.

"Well," Sara began, "we did have a particular *chessed* project in mind for today."

"Oh?" Binny questioned.

"And," I impulsively added, "I think it would be very beneficial to have Aviva tag along."

"And what is this *chessed* act that you would like to do?" Binny asked again.

"Yesterday, when we were captured during the counselors' hunt," Sara said, framing her words carefully, "we noticed the girls from the various bunks running across Tante's garden indiscriminately. They stepped all over her seeds and plants and flowers. We figured we would see what we could do about setting the garden back in order again."

Binny nodded.

"That's a great idea," she said. "And working close to nature and not having anyone expect anything from her might give Aviva an incentive to talk. Well, good luck!"

We entered the dining room and proceeded to our table. The interplay at breakfast seemed to shift around me as if I was in a dream. I couldn't erase the eerie sounds I had heard emanating from Tante's cottage. Maybe my ears had tricked me? Perhaps they were really sounds of a wounded animal coming from *behind* the cottage? Deep down, I knew this was just wishful thinking.

After *bentching, shiur* and clean-up, Binny introduced us to Aviva. I couldn't take my eyes off of her. Every single feature in her face was perfection. Golden curls bounced loosely around her heart-shaped face. Her large blue eyes were fringed with long, dark eyelashes. She had a perfect button nose and bright red lips that looked painted on. When she gave us her full smile, her eyes sparkled and her deep dimples and perfect white teeth added to her charm. Aviva indeed looked like a perfect child. But why wouldn't she talk?

My heart pounded with the responsibility of taking on this important task. Sara, however, decided to treat Aviva as one of her sisters.

"Come on," she said, as she took Aviva's hand. "We're off to do a *mitzvah*."

Sara began singing and skipping and dancing, and the only option left for me was to follow along.

"Hey, wait for me!" I shouted, trying to catch up. "Don't hog the *mitzvah* for yourselves."

We arrived at the pathway to Tante's cottage. Instinctively, Sara and I drew back, afraid of what awaited us behind the doors. I felt Aviva's hand pulling us impatiently forward. Diffidently, we approached the porch.

The steps creaked as we climbed them in a single file. On the porch, the old wooden slats contributed their own music. Could this be what we had heard last night?

Sara opened the screen door and raised her hand to knock on the old wooden door. The paint on the door was peeling.

"I guess when we finish our *chessed* job of cleaning up the garden, we could volunteer to repaint the bungalow," I suggested.

Sara turned towards me and nodded, and at that moment, the front door opened a crack.

"What can I do for you?" Tante politely inquired.

Her pleasant voice shocked me. So did her neat and proper appearance. I hardly believed this was the same Tante who had acted so strangely in the garden the previous day.

Sara did not act at all surprised. I guess she was used to Tante's different moods and ways of dress.

"Could we come in and speak with you for a few minutes?" Sara asked, at the same time trying to edge herself into Tante's kitchen.

Her efforts were doomed to failure. Tante came outside and closed the door firmly behind her, effectively thwarting our attempt to enter Tante's kitchen and discover the source of the moans.

Tante sat down on one of the porch steps and indicated that we should follow suit.

"Now," she repeated, seeming a little more at ease. "What can I do for you?"

Sara saw we would not be able to investigate the interior, so she repeated our alibi.

"We have two activities every day which we are supposed to devote to doing chessed," Sara began.

Tante nodded.

"We noticed what happened yesterday," Sara continued.

Tante looked at us with a puzzled expression. I wondered if she was trying to hide something or if she really did not remember what had happened.

"Nothing unusual happened," Tante shook her head in denial.

Then, as if she suddenly remembered, her face seemed to close up and her voice became very cautious.

"What did you girls see?" she asked suspiciously.

Sara and I exchanged glances. Was Tante trying to hide the fact she had acted in a bizarre fashion yesterday? Was she afraid we would accuse her of being senile?

"We saw the girls from the younger bunks ruining your garden," I said.

"We know how hard you must have worked on your garden," Sara added. "And so we decided to volunteer to work in your garden and repair the damage."

"Oh," Tante replied, and a great sigh of relief escaped her. "I thought you meant . . ."

But Tante did not finish her statement. She seemed to hear something undetectable to our ears and quickly rose to her feet. We immediately followed suit.

"Sure," she said and swept her arm to indicate the whole garden. "Do whatever you want. I'm glad to see young girls thinking about doing *chessed* and interested in learning this *midah* thoroughly."

Distractedly, she proceeded into her cottage and slammed the door behind her. I looked immediately at Sara, inquiring silently into her thoughts.

Tante's door reopened, and Tante leaned her head out. She smiled in a free-spirited manner.

"And thank you for thinking about doing this *chessed* for me," she called out.

Sara and I smiled at Tante's eccentric manner.

"I'm beginning to like the old lady," I said.

"I know," Sara answered. "Even I'm beginning to feel a

little bit guilty about what we are doing. But not too much."

"What are we doing?" I asked, although I already knew the response I would receive.

"Why, spying, of course," Sara replied with a shrug, as if this was a normal activity in our everyday lives.

❧ **4** ❧

THE TORTURED VICTIM

We gardened with a gusto, and Aviva participated actively in our work. I loved to garden, having always helped my mother when she planted her tomatoes and zucchini. I personally preferred nurturing flowers and bushes, but I loved anything that grew.

Sara, though, seemed to enjoy things that moved. After about one hour of hard work, I found that although Aviva and I were working diligently side by side, Sara had wandered off and was peering intently at Tante's window.

I shrugged and continued working. All the while, I explained to Aviva what I was doing, keeping up an endless current of conversation. I wished she would respond

to me, but she only nodded her head, indicating she understood what I was saying.

The hot sun beat down on my back. My ponytail, which had bounced jubilantly in the morning, hung limply down my back. I raised myself to my feet, straightened my back and stretched. Aviva, my shadow, followed me exactly.

I looked at the patch of ground we had just finished weeding. We had transplanted the plants that had been trampled the day before. I nodded at my silent partner. It was a good morning's work. Then I looked at Sara. I had been so intent on my task I had not realized that Sara had positioned herself below the open window.

I silently questioned her. Sara shook her head in the negative. There was nothing new to report.

I thought about our other goal in working on the garden. So far I had not found anything I could describe as precious. There were no jewels buried there, no treasure. And there were certainly no diamonds buried in the spots where we had been working.

Aviva took my hand and pulled it to get my attention. She looked straight at my eyes. Her voice had not been heard, but I distinctly knew Aviva was telling me in her silent way that she was thirsty.

"I'll ask Tante for a drink," I suggested to Aviva, indicating the front porch door.

Aviva did not wait for me to finish the sentence. She hurriedly skipped up the steps, knocked at the front door and opened it.

I was shocked at the scene that confronted me. A woman was sitting in a wheel chair, her left arm hanging limply at her side. Connected to the arm was a white snakelike tube. The tube was linked to a bottle of clear liquid. The woman was obviously very ill. She could hardly hold her head straight, and it rolled dizzily on her weak neck as we watched in silence. As we became unbidden witnesses, we saw Tante raise her hand and hit her victim roughly, not once, not twice, but three times!

We must have gasped, because Tante suddenly turned around and encountered her audience. She gave no defense. She did not even yell at us. She had no chance. As she moved toward where we were standing, Sara and I both grabbed Aviva by her small pudgy fingers and quickly fled from the scene.

We didn't stop until we reached the grassy lawn in front of the bunks. We could vaguely see Tante standing at the doorway in the distance. Her shoulders seemed slumped with a heavy burden.

No wonder, I thought to myself. I also would be upset if I was caught torturing a sick invalid incapable of defense. And this was the Tante who lectures people about doing *chessed*?

🌼 **5** 🌼

NIGHT ACTIVITY

"I don't understand her," Sara said.

"Neither do I," I agreed.

We were walking towards the dining room after *davening Minchah*. We had spent the rest of the day participating in our *ohel's* activities. But although we were going through the motions of actively joining the activities, our minds were definitely on the incident of the morning.

As soon as we had returned from Tante, we had washed up and had taken care of Aviva. We had both agreed that it was a good thing Aviva wasn't able to talk. We didn't want the whole camp to find out what had happened.

As we walked towards the dining room for supper, we

reviewed what had happened and tried to make some sense of it.

"It's just not consistent with the type of person you described to me," I insisted. "A woman who gave of herself so generously that the camp gives her a cottage here permanently just wouldn't act in such a manner. It doesn't make sense!"

"Yes," Sara admitted. "It seems to be a case of a person with a split personality."

"What do you mean?" I questioned.

"Well, one minute Tante acts like a kind and gentle soul, intent on doing acts of kindness," Sara explained. "And then, within twenty-four hours, she is beating an obviously ill woman."

"Do you think . . .?" I hesitated to ask the question that was lurking in my mind.

"Do I think what?" Sara prompted me impatiently.

"Well, maybe Tante is mentally disturbed," I ventured a guess. "Maybe she enjoys hitting people."

"Hey," Sara remarked with a mirthless laugh. "You're beginning to sound like me." She shook her head in denial. "It just sounds too melodramatic. I can't believe things like that happen in real life. You read about personalities such as you are describing in books. They really don't exist."

"I know," I answered. "*Frum* people with a Torah background would never be so sadistic."

I hesitated a moment as we came abreast of some of our friends. I let the conversation buzz around us, as we passed the group.

"Do you think we should speak to Rabbi Rubin, the camp director," I asked Sara.

"I don't know," she answered. "I usually jump to conclusions which prove wrong. Maybe we should just continue to observe things."

I agreed with Sara that we should remain quiet about the incident and continue to keep Tante under surveillance. Yet, the picture of that pathetic figure in the wheelchair being slapped and manhandled could not be easily dismissed from my memory.

Would I be endangering the victim by not reporting Tante's bizarre behavior?

I was in a quandary. Maybe I was judging Tante too harshly. But no. I could not deny what my eyes had seen. Tante had definitely hit the woman.

I could see these thoughts going through Sara's mind as well. She was acting completely distracted. What was the proper thing for us to do?

"I know," Sara said softly, "that if a teacher suspects a child has been physically abused, the teacher is supposed to report it."

"But this is not school," I reminded Sara. "And besides, that lady was not a child."

"That's true," said Sara. "But was she well enough to defend herself?"

"No, that was a very sick woman in Tante's bungalow," I added thoughtfully. "But what if there is another explanation for what we saw? Then we'd look pretty foolish if we reported it."

"All right, then let's just keep an eye on things," Sara

said. "If we are always around, perhaps Tante will be afraid to beat the sick lady again."

"That's a good idea," I said. "And besides, now that Tante knows we caught her in the act, she will probably think twice before she beats anyone another time."

We proceeded into the dining room and were enthusiastically greeted by Aviva. Enthusiastically? Well, although no words passed her lips, Aviva's hugs and kisses were definitely not of a passive nature.

I hugged Aviva back. She was such a gentle child, with such a sweet nature. I hoped she had not been harmed by what she had seen. I watched her as she skipped back to her own group.

Binny elbowed me with a smile of satisfaction on her face.

"I knew I made the right choice in you, Bracha," she said. "Aviva has really taken to you."

I smiled shyly and began to blush furiously.

"She's so adorable," I answered. "We do get along great together. And I'm also gaining a lot from this companionship."

We washed and sat down to eat supper. The campers were almost up to *bentching* and were singing with gusto. I had pushed my thoughts of Tante and her guest to the back of my mind.

Suddenly, the lights in the dining room blinked off and then on again. The little children began to scream but were immediately pacified by their counselors. I laughed knowingly to myself, and I saw my friends doing the same. The lights blinked off and on again, and we all giggled.

"Just another breakout for some night activity," Naomi wisely stated.

After a few minutes, the lights ceased flickering, and calm reigned once again in the dining room. We all waited anxiously for the announcement of the night activity.

"Hey," Rena cried. "What is going on here? I was just about to go down to the *ohel* when the lights flickered off and on. I was afraid I would miss something, so I decided not to go."

Just as Rena finished saying her words, the lights again flickered off and on, but this time they flickered off again and stayed off. I looked out the large dining room window and saw that the dining room was not the only place that was darkened. The whole camp was without lights, and it was very hard to see what was happening outside in the gathering dusk.

I felt someone move right near me. It was Sara. As everyone was busy discussing theories as to why the lights had gone out and what type of night activity would be "broken out," Sara slipped out the door.

I tried to envision where she could be going. As I passively listened to the conversations going on around me, I felt Sara slip back into the seat next to me.

"I was just out on the porch," she whispered. "I think I saw something going on near Tante's cottage. Come quickly."

As unobtrusively as possible, I followed her out to the dining room porch.

"Be quick and quiet," she ordered. "I suspect that something very interesting is going on."

She quickly pulled me by the hand and led me towards the direction of the main road.

It was very hard to run. We were going downhill, and we could hardly see where we were going. There was a mist in the air, which made everything appear cloaked in a thick covering.

"Slow down," I said to Sara. "I can't see anything!"

Sara grabbed my hand and we ran together. I tripped over stones and branches. I wanted to stop, but Sara was determined to forge ahead.

"Here," she said. "We've arrived."

She was whispering, and now I knew why.

The lights had not flickered and gone out because of any break-out for a silly night activity. Both Sara and I knew now why somebody had been fiddling with the lights. The purpose had been to keep all the campers and counselors up the hill in the dining room. They wanted nobody down by the road, as we were standing now. It was extremely important that nobody see what we were observing.

We were standing on the edge of the road, completely hidden by the trees. We were a little to the side of Tante's cottage. Parked in front of the cottage was a large official car. I gasped when I recognized it as an ambulance.

We had arrived just in time to see the doors to the ambulance being shut. One emergency medical technician quickly ran to the driver's side of the ambulance, hurriedly started the engine and drove off in a burst of speed. I saw Tante quickly enter her car and set off after the ambulance.

Sara and I stood rooted to our spot.

"Is that the sick lady in the ambulance?" I ventured to guess.

"I hope she's all right," Sara answered hesitantly.

"What is going on?" we both wondered together. "What is going on?"

6

A BOND IS FORMED

The days drifted into weeks. Sara and I continued our observation of Tante and her activities. We were really perplexed by the continuous activity in Tante's cottage.

"Did she always have so many guests?" I asked Sara at least twenty times in that first month of camp.

Each time I questioned Sara she tried very hard to remember, but her conclusion was always the same.

"I just don't remember," Sara would say. "Tante was always just a fixture in Camp Rivkah. I don't remember even noticing her that much during previous years."

Aviva, Sara and I continued working on the garden, and Tante never said a word to us about the incident with the invalid, nor we to her.

At first, we had started doing this chore temporarily to repair the damage done during the counselor hunt. But as the days of the summer progressed, we found we enjoyed working in the garden. We liked the companionship and privacy it gave us.

You see, camp is a lot of fun. You meet new girls and make new friends. But you are constantly living together in the same room and under the same roof with fifteen or so other girls.

Oh, there are lots of benefits to camp life. I'm the first to agree. I *love* camp. There's constant partying, and you are never lonely. But, well, privacy is also very precious. That's why I liked those morning activities where Sara, Aviva and I could work in Tante's garden.

Sara and I had developed such a close friendship that we never had to apologize for being moody. If we felt like talking, we did. If Sara wanted to explore and I was also in the mood, we did. And if I felt like just sorting out my thoughts in the seclusion of the garden, I could do that, too.

And what was happening with Aviva all this time? Well, nothing . . . and everything. Aviva still hadn't said a word to us, but we loved her. It was funny. Aviva was not much more than half our age, but we talked to her as if she was our best friend. She just fit in so well that when we returned her to her *ohel* after the *chessed* activities, I would feel a twinge of emptiness.

Oh, don't get me wrong. Aviva would skip right back to her friends, smiling and happy. Sara and I would also return to our more sophisticated activities. It's just that Aviva had made a deep mark on us, and as the days flowed into weeks without any changes in her speech, we began to feel disheartened. We had been so sure we would be the instruments used to perform Aviva's verbal miracle, but nothing was happening.

7

LET THE SUNSHINE IN

I awoke to the sounds of rain drumming on the rooftop. The room was still dark, and I was sure that *boker tov* had not yet been announced. I lay back on my pillow, crisscrossing my fingers behind my head, and gazed up at the top bunk bed, savoring the quiet moments before the camp would awaken.

It seemed to have been raining for most of the night. The steady downpour did not sound as if it was ready to abate. I wondered what our day's activities would be.

I didn't have too long to wait.

"*Boker tov*, Machaneh Rivkah, *boker tov*," Ruchie began her warm morning address.

"How could she sound so cheerful," Naomi groaned, "on such a dismal morning?"

"Come on," Sara chirped from her nest above me. "If it's raining outside, then it's our job to let the sunshine in. I've got a great idea."

Sara was notorious for her ideas. Sometimes, they were really successful. Sometimes, they would backfire and get us all into trouble. But her ideas always deserved an A for originality.

As soon as we were dressed, we gathered around Sara, and she explained her idea to us. We all enthusiastically agreed to her suggestions. As soon as we finished *davening* on the porch, as we had been instructed, we began to prepare our surprise.

Naomi was in charge of getting the arts and crafts supplies. She was going to take Tova and Layah with her. They dressed in raincoats, and armed with giant garbage bags, they went to raid the supply closet. As they were about to leave the *ohel* laden with instructions and long lists, they were stopped at the doorway by Binny.

"Okay," she said, hands on her hips. "What is all the excitement about?"

She was answered with guilty looks and absolute silence.

"Come on," Binny prodded, tapping her foot on the ground, pretending to be impatient. "What's up? You know you can't fool me."

We all turned to Sara, because she had the most nerve and could best explain her plan to Binny.

Binny listened intently, but we could not discern by

looking at her face whether she approved of the plan. When Sara finished her explanation, Binny sat thoughtfully on the edge of her bed. We all waited expectantly. Suddenly, her face lit up.

"If you girls can wait just five minutes," she said, "I know how you can have your surprise and not get in trouble at the same time."

Binny quickly ran out of the *ohel*, and we sat around waiting for her return.

"You don't think they will disapprove, will they?" Tova asked anxiously.

"No, I doubt it," Naomi answered.

"But it sure takes the fun out of something when it isn't done spontaneously," Sara complained.

Sara glanced at me. I tried to hide my relief that Binny had walked in on our plans. I am such a coward, and I hate to do anything which might get me into trouble. Sara had to take out her frustration in waiting, so she threw a pillow at me.

I retaliated. They don't call me Bracha the Bomb for nothing, and I hit her smack on target. It pays to be such an excellent player in *machanayim*. The pillow fight would have erupted into a full-fledged war, except that we were interrupted by Binny's stormy entrance into our room.

"It's all set!" Binny exclaimed breathlessly as she shook herself out of her sopping wet raincoat. "You're on."

With a frenzy, we prepared.

Naomi and her committee went to the supply closet. Sara, myself and a few other girls went to the sports closet. The rest of the girls raided their cubbies and brought out anything and everything that was appropriate for carrying out our plan.

As I worked in the sports closet, filling the list that had been handed to me, I noticed Sara disappear. Oh well, I shrugged to myself. She's probably investigating Tante's cottage, and she'll fill me in when she is ready. As I thought about the activity ahead, though, my thoughts of Sara and her disappearance settled into the back of my mind.

Soon Sara was back, and we all carried our load to the *ohel*.

Then the preparations really began. We all dressed in different radiant, brightly colored costumes. We specifically used as much yellow as possible. Then tying yellow streamers and yellow ribbons around our wrists and feet and pinning yellow crowns on our heads and yellow balloons on any other open area, we giggled and learned our song by heart.

"Let the sunshine in.
Let the sunshine in.
Don't be sad 'cause of the rain.
This is no time to complain.
Every tear you should erase.
Bring a smile to your face.
Let the sunshine in."

Then we covered ourselves with the giant garbage bags and sneaked towards the dining room.

The rest of the campers were just finishing their breakfast. We took out the roller skates I had helped borrow from the sports closet and put them on. Then with Sara leading the way and holding on to a long colorful ribbon, we made a snakelike line and roller skated into the dining room singing our song.

At first, we were greeted with absolute silence. I began to have doubts if we were doing a smart thing. But as we continued to weave around the tables and benches, the children started to clap and tried to learn the song and sing along with us.

Suddenly, Sara, who was at the head of the line, stopped moving. We all piled up on top of one another and started laughing.

"Give me a hand," Sara said to one of the counselors, as she endeavored to stand on top of one of the chairs.

"You're nuts," I said to her. "You're liable to fall and hurt yourself."

But daring Sara didn't seem to hear me.

Standing on top of the chair, she began to do aerobics in time to the tune. Soon, she had the whole camp singing the song and copying her hand motions, and indeed, it looked like the sun had definitely been permitted to shine into the dining room.

Suddenly, there was a shout from one of the counselors near the window.

"Hey, AJCs, you've worked a miracle!" she whooped. "It stopped raining, and the sun is beginning to slip out!"

As the camp cheered, Sara seemed disappointed that the attention had been diverted from her. She attempted to leap down from her chair, expecting to land upright on the floor.

Under normal circumstances, Sara probably would have landed upright even though she was wearing roller skates. But this time, she lost her balance, and before I could prevent it from happening, Sara lay sprawled on the floor. Her left foot was extended in a very uncomfortable-looking angle. Her face turned white, her eyes grew larger and the freckles stood out on her nose. My brave friend Sara tried to hold herself back from crying.

I quickly ran to her and took the roller skates off her feet. The dining room was in a great uproar. I saw Binny rush over and heard Ruchie trying to maintain order. The nurse was immediately at Sara's side, and after a very quick examination, she warned us not to move her.

"I'm going to call Hatzalah," she said. "I think the foot is broken."

I held Sara's hand and tried to comfort her, but for some reason, I felt Sara was trying to comfort me.

Ruchie had gotten the dining room quiet. She quickly started the camp *bentching*. The atmosphere was thick with concern for Sara.

Almost immediately after *bentching*, we heard the Hatzalah ambulance siren. The emergency medical technicians came rushing in. A Hatzalah squad member looked at Sara's leg and confirmed what we all suspected.

"The foot looks broken," he said. "I'm going to take you to the hospital for x-rays."

The whole scene seemed like an act from a play. These things don't really happen in real life, I said to myself. I couldn't believe my vibrant and vivacious friend Sara would break her leg and be out of commission for the rest of the summer. If Sara wouldn't be up and moving around, she would be so bored. I looked at her in despair. Strangely enough, Sara didn't look too upset. She winked at me and then, as she was lifted on the stretcher by the nurse and some counselors, she bravely began to sing.

"Let the sunshine in.
Let the sunshine in."

Nobody sang along with her. We all admired her spirit and then we saw she had changed the words of the song.

"Don't be sad because of the rain.
This is no time to complain."

And then, Sara jumped from the stretcher and climbed back on to the chair, her foot obviously not hurting her in the least. The heads and Binny and Sara all sang out with great spirit.

"This whole accident was just the way,
That we're breaking out—
FIELD DAY!"

8

GESHEM AND SHEMESH

I couldn't believe the magnificent acting Sara had done. She had certainly looked like she had broken her foot. But it was all a preplanned method to break out Field Day.

I was finally able to get Sara to myself. Everyone was surrounding her, talking about the breakout, and I found it hard to corner her and speak to the celebrity privately. Finally, Ruchie got the camp quiet and began to discuss the rules of Field Day, and Sara approached me.

"I'm sorry I didn't tell you what was going on," Sara apologized.

I had been hurt that I wasn't taken into her confidence,

but after Sara's apology, I was embarrassed at my feelings.

"It's okay," I said with a shrug. "But how long has this been planned?"

"Just today," Sara answered. "You have to understand how things in this camp are run."

I really didn't understand. I was used to everything being pre-planned by staff members and with no campers being taken into their confidence.

"Camp Rivkah is a very family oriented camp," Sara explained. "We try to enforce the idea that everyone is smart enough and bright enough to originate suggestions. When Binny heard about our plans for raiding the dining room, she immediately thought of it as a break-out for Field Day. She confided in Ruchie, and this was the result."

It was a good feeling that everyone had the opportunity to contribute something to camp spirit.

"But didn't the heads have another break-out planned for Field Day?"

"I guess so," Sara replied. "But this one just fell into their laps." She looked at the foot that was supposed to have been broken. "In a manner of speaking, I guess. Shhh. Let's find out what team we're on."

Sara's revelations had given me a lot to think about. Surveying the dining room, I saw there was an atmosphere prevailing I had not seen in any other camp. Although it was now Field Day, and there would be a lot of competition, there was a spirit of excitement and, believe it or not, unity.

"Okay," I heard Ruchie addressing the camp. "Since

this whole break-out had to do with the rain and the sun, the two teams are naturally being named Team Geshem and Team Shemesh."

Ruchie's announcement was met with cheers.

"And of course," Ruchie continued, "the color for Team Geshem is blue and the color of Team Shemesh is yellow."

These words were also greeted with cheers. I began to feel like an observer rather than a participant. Ruchie's next announcement, however, brought me right back to reality.

"The captains of Team Shemesh are Galli and Layah," she said.

We all cheered as they blushingly walked to the front of the dining room.

"And the captains of Team Geshem are Rivky and Bracha," she added.

I stood there rooted to the spot. I was stunned. I didn't want to be captain of Field Day. I am a worker, not a leader. I couldn't move.

My bunkmates pushed me forward, and I soon found myself standing next to Sara's sister Rivky in front of the whole dining room. I felt everyone looking at me, and I blushed in embarrassment.

"Let me explain how we divide up the camp," Ruchie continued. "All the girls whose names begin with the letters *alef* to *kof* are on Team Geshem. And all the girls whose names begin with the letters *lamed* to *tof* are on Team Shemesh."

I looked at Sara. She would be on the other team. How

was I ever going to get through the next twenty four hours?

Rivky took me to the side and started walking towards the arts and crafts room. That was to be Team Geshem's headquarters.

"Calm down," Rivky said.

"You mean it's so obvious I'm a physical wreck?" I asked.

"Don't worry about anything," Rivky continued. "Field Day in Camp Rivkah is very different from Field Days in other camps."

"What do you mean?" I asked.

Rivky unfolded the sheet of paper that listed the competitions for Field Day. I sighed in relief when I realized this wasn't going to be a mini Color War.

"All the activities throughout the day are sports activities," Rivky explained. "Each camper competes within her own bunk. The night activity is comedy races. Overnight, we get to work on a banner depicting our theme. We can present the banner in whatever way we see fit, by singing or with music or even a dramatic presentation. That is done right after breakfast in the social hall."

I looked at Rivky questioningly. Usually, the banner was left as the last presentation. This gave the team plenty of time to create a masterpiece. Rivky obviously understood my puzzlement, because she answered my unspoken question.

"The whole idea of our Field Day is to have fun in a competitive manner," she said. "The camp feels that one night of frenzied work is usually sufficient to provide a nice banner. They know lack of sleep tends to get everyone edgy and short of temper. It would take away from the unity for which our camp is famous. It would bring out too many bad *midos* that are certainly not the goal of the Field Day.

"Tomorrow morning, after the banner is presented, the younger campers have competitive races at the pool. The AJCs will continue doing their *chessed* activities. As you probably noticed, *chessed* is one activity in Camp Rivkah that is a priority over every other activity. Then comes the marathon race."

"What is that?" I asked.

"Oh, that's the most fun of all."

As Rivky explained it to me, I laughingly pictured the possible disastrous results.

"I can tell," I said, finally breathing normally, "that Field Day is really a fun day in Camp Rivkah."

❦ **9** ❦

THE THIRD HARMONY

I was surprised that although Field Day was a competitive day complete with numerous new activities, certain activities did not change. Rivky had been right. The AJCs still had the regular morning *chessed* program. I was glad to see Sara.

We were walking towards Tante's cottage, with Aviva dancing and skipping in between us. The sun was shining brightly, in extreme contrast to the dull and dark awakening of this morning.

"I feel so guilty," I said to Sara. "Why am I walking through the still damp grass to work in Tante's garden? I should be holed up in the arts and crafts building plotting my strategy for Field Day."

Sara smiled tolerantly.

"I told you Camp Rivkah is different from any other camp you might have attended," Sara explained. "The camp was started with one frame of thought in mind. It is a summer extension of our school year *chinuch*. Every action and every camp activity is reviewed seriously before it is accepted into the camp mold."

"Yes," I agreed half-heartedly. "But what criteria are used to determine whether or not an activity is appropriate for Camp Rivkah?"

"Simple," Sara answered. "The directors are constantly questioning the purpose behind each action. If the competition helps develop a good *midah*, then it is permitted to be used. And no matter what, if there is any question about an activity, then a *shaylah* is asked."

I reviewed that information for a few moments.

"So what is beneficial about a Field Day?" I questioned. "It's true that I love sports. But *midah*-wise, what can we gain from a Field Day?"

I saw my question had puzzled Sara.

"Look," Sara finally said. "Let's take each activity as it comes. You'll see. I won't even have to explain it to you. You'll see for yourself how every single action in Camp Rivkah helps work towards the goal of developing true Bais Yaakov girls with proper *Bnos Yisrael midos tovos*."

I nodded. I was a little doubtful if Sara could prove to me that Camp Rivkah was so-o-o unique. But I certainly was prepared to observe Field Day and accept her claims if need be.

"I truly hope you are right," I admitted.

We arrived at Tante's garden.

"I hope the ground isn't too wet to work with," I said to Aviva.

Aviva just nodded her head, took the bag of gardening tools from my hand, and skipped to the spot in the garden where we had left off.

The earth was soft and slightly muddy, but the night's rain had made the soil more pliable and easier to work with. We set ourselves to task, our heads bent over in concentration. Sara and I exchanged comments above Aviva's head. She did not seem to mind not contributing to the conversation but just steadfastly continued to work.

"Boy," Sara exclaimed, sitting back to take a short rest. "The sun is really beating down on us. How long have we been working?"

I also stopped digging for a minute and wiped my forehead with my muddy hand.

"Only about an hour," I answered. "We still have another activity left to go."

"I feel like I'm a slave in Egypt," Sara joked.

I playfully shoved her.

"Okay, slave," I said with a laugh "Back to work!"

Sara started to sing a *Pesach* song depicting *Bnei Yisrael's* slavery in Egypt. In a minute, I had joined in with harmony. We continued to work and sing . . . and that was when the miracle occurred.

As Sara sang the alto part of the song, and I harmonized with the soprano tune, we both heard a third voice, clear as a bell, singing a three-part harmony.

Sara and I both stopped working in shock, but as we sat, with our bodies frozen, our voices continued to sing.

The third voice also continued the melodic harmony, oblivious to us. We looked at each other, and then we looked at Aviva.

The little eight-year-old girl, who had not spoken a word for such a long time, was harmonizing the song with us.

Okay, it was true. There were no words to her harmony. But we were the first people in Camp Rivkah, and possibly in the whole world, who had heard Aviva's voice in the past four years.

It was as beautiful and as clear as the voices of the birds who were now accompanying her in the garden.

❧ **10** ❧

A MUD BATH

We were shocked, but we slowly continued to work. We had stopped singing, and so had Aviva. Silently, Sara and I exchanged looks, and very casually we began to pack up our tools.

"Come on, Aviva," I said, trying hard not to let my voice shake. "We have to stop gardening a little earlier today. We're all muddy, and we have to clean ourselves up."

Aviva, always obedient, stopped her work immediately and smiled a brilliant smile.

"Too bad you're on Team Geshem, Aviva," Sara commented. "Your smile is so radiant it puts the *shemesh* to shame."

"Hey, that's a good idea," I kidded Sara. "Maybe we'll use Aviva as our team mascot to help put Team Shemesh to shame."

Sara playfully began to run after me.

"Oh, no, you don't," I teased as I escaped her clutches. "You can't catch me."

Sara lunged towards me. I attempted to dodge her, but I missed seeing the puddle of mud underneath the tree.

"Oh, no," I shrieked as I felt myself falling.

I grabbed onto Sara to steady myself, but it didn't help. Within seconds, Sara and I were both half sitting and half lying in a big mud bath. I took one look at Sara and began to giggle.

"You've got about a million new freckles," I choked out, pointing at her face.

Sara couldn't answer my taunt. She was too busy laughing and pointing at me.

"Well, it must be the newest style," I shrugged as I attempted to stand up. "It's fashionable to take a mud bath for healthy skin."

As we laughingly regained our balance, Aviva's clear voice was heard again. She was laughing. Up until now she had only smiled at us. Today, she even laughed with us.

"I guess we do look kind of funny," Sara commented.

"I'm really sorry I pulled you down," I sheepishly apologized.

"Who cares?" Sara shrugged it off. "That was fun."

As we walked back to our *ohel* to take showers, we were pointed at by half of the camp.

"Boy," Sara said. "Believe it or not, but you can actually see your face turning red even under all the mud."

As usual, I was blushing from the embarrassment of being noticed.

We deposited Aviva with her bunk and quickly rushed to take showers. It was a relief to be able to disappear into anonymity again, the result of a quick and cleansing shower.

As planned, Sara and I met Binny right before wash-up for lunch.

"You had better sit down," Sara warned Binny after we led her to a shady bench under the trees.

"What's up, you two?" Binny asked. "If I didn't see those smiles of yours lurking at the corners of your mouths, I would say you have some very mysterious and solemn news to tell me."

"We do," I nodded, trying not to blurt out the good news.

But both Sara and I found our exciting information much too good to keep a secret. We both started talking at once.

"Aviva sang," I said.

"Aviva laughed," Sara said at the same exact time.

"Whoa," Binny stopped us in our tracks. "Did I hear you correctly?" She looked at me. "Did you just say that you heard Aviva sing?"

I nodded.

"She didn't sing any words," I added. "But she was definitely singing a tune, and the sounds were coming out of her throat."

"And how about you, Sara?" Binny asked. "Did you also hear Aviva laugh?"

"Yes," Sara answered excitedly. "Her laughter was sweet and clear and beautiful . . . like . . . like . . . just like a bell."

"You're so poetic," I teased Sara, but Binny did not seem to hear me. She was looking out in the distance and talking to herself.

"The doctors were right," she whispered quietly. "There *is nothing wrong* with Aviva's vocal chords or her voice. For some reason, she just hasn't wanted to talk."

Binny faced us again.

"Do you know?" she said to us. "I think you two are the only people in the world who have heard Aviva's voice in the past couple of years."

Sara and I nodded. The thought had definitely crossed our minds.

"I'm going to call up my mother right now," Binny said. "This is the most exciting news I can give her."

I felt elated. I couldn't believe our companionship with Aviva had helped bring about this miracle.

"I don't think you should, Binny," Sara said.

"Why not?" I asked. I wanted the world to know the part we had played in Aviva's recovery.

"Because although the singing and laughing is a step in the right direction," Sara continued, "it is not actually talking. I think we should wait a while and see if these miracles continue to occur."

Although I was a little disappointed, I agreed with Sara's decision.

"It's true," I added to Binny. "Aviva has not spoken for many years. We have to let her get used to the novelty so she doesn't clam up again."

"You're right," Binny agreed. "And she still hasn't said any words yet. Maybe by the time visiting day comes around Aviva will really be communicating."

As we lined up for lunch, we noticed that each *ohel* was lined up in two separate lines, one for Team Geshem and the other for Team Shemesh. I caught Rivky's eye and saw her beckoning me.

"Have you been thinking of an idea for a banner?" she asked me.

I explained to her what had happened this morning during our *chessed* project.

"At first, I thought I would have time to think while working in the garden," I said. "But once Sara and I started talking, we found we couldn't stop. And then came Aviva's miracle."

"I don't blame you for being distracted," Rivky said. "But even without your kind of morning, I couldn't come up with any ideas. Right after lunch, we have to get a group together just to develop ideas."

We agreed to meet at the arts and crafts building after lunch.

I thoughtfully walked back to my place on line. Was it just Rivky Goodman's personality not to get tense or nervous? Why wasn't she short-tempered and aggravated that I had spent my morning with Aviva and having a mud party? Wouldn't other heads of Field Day in other camps have been disgusted with me? Wouldn't they have yelled at me and embarrassed me? Was it just Rivky's way? Or was this an example of Sara's description of Field Day in Camp Rivkah? Did people really count more than activities and Field Days and competitions and Color War?

❀ **11** ❀

BANNERS AND BATHS

After lunch, we met in the arts and crafts building. Art was not my forte, and I could see I was going to have a hard time coming up with good suggestions. Of course, part of my problem was that I felt intimidated by all the counselors. After all, I was just a lowly AJC. But I must admit I still had lots of fun.

We were lying all over the floor of the arts and crafts room, playing tapes on the tape recorder, eating popcorn and just generally shmoozing. Why weren't the girls nervous? I thought by now somebody would have come up with a suggestion, and we would at least begin working on the banner. The atmosphere, though, was very casual, and nobody seemed disturbed.

"Hey, I've got a great idea," Gila said. "Let's have an Indian rain dance."

"Yeah, that's fantastic."

And with general approval, Gila started writing a cheer to use for the comedy races during night activity.

"But we need a banner," I groaned.

"Boy, are you a worrier," Rivky said. "Don't despair. Somebody will come up with something."

Suddenly, I found Rivky looking at me in a very familiar way. Rivky was beginning to remind me of Sara.

"Oh, no," I began to complain audibly. "You've got a Sara look on you. What are you cooking up, Rivky?"

"Why don't we use you in our theme?" Rivky suggested.

I noticed all the girls suddenly stop working. They all looked at me, nodding their heads thoughtfully.

"Yeah," Devorah said. "She could make our whole theme. You sing, don't you?"

I found myself blushing furiously. I had absolutely no idea about what was going on. How could I be part of the theme?

"Yes," Rivky persisted. "Bracha could lead us into the dining hall while we carry the banner. It will definitely give an added dimension to our theme."

"And if she sings the theme song as beautifully as I heard she can—" Devorah excitedly added.

"But what is the theme song?" I interrupted, completely baffled. "And what is our theme for the banner? And what do I have to do with it?"

All the girls looked at me in disbelief. But I really had no idea as to what they meant. I was very embarrassed and wished I could find a hole in which to hide. Was this how Sara referred to Camp Rivkah—a place full of *midos*? But I kicked myself as I thought badly of the girls, since they really thought I was putting one over on them.

"Bracha," Rivky gently explained. "We thought you understood and you were just teasing us. Our theme is a play on your name."

"My name?" I questioned, and then I began to understand. "Ohhh, I see."

"That's right," Rivky nodded, and to erase all doubts from my mind, she explained further. "Our theme will be *Gishmei Bracha*. It's a play on your name. But what we will really be depicting is the times when we will merit the *Gishmei Bracha*, the times of *Mashiach*."

I nodded my head and thanked Rivky for explaining it to me. How could I have possibly thought Rivky would intentionally embarrass me? I promised myself I would make it up to her by never doubting her again.

Then the real work began. As I said before, I don't know how to draw, so I quickly dismissed myself from that part of the preparations. But I do like to write, and when the work on the theme song began, I found myself joining that group.

We had lots of fun. The girls all contributed something to the theme song. And even though some of the suggestions might not have been the best, nobody was ridiculed or insulted. Each girl was encouraged to participate in some way to the final result.

I sat back and silently observed the girls working

together with such camaraderie. I was extremely impressed. Even though this was a competitive day, we had all been working with positive thoughts in our minds. Not once had a suggestion come forth to put down or ridicule the other team. Maybe Sara was right. Maybe by working on developing *midos tovos* all the time, in school and also during summer vacation, we could develop into true *Bnos Yisrael*.

"Hurry up!" Rivky exclaimed. "It's already *Minchah* time. Let's see if we could get our team to *Shul* on time. Remember, Gila, we have to teach them your Indian rain dance cheer before night activity."

I was having a great time. Field Day at Camp Rivkah, although different, was definitely fun.

After supper, we all gathered in the social hall for races. The sports counselors had arranged everything, and we all sat in our places on opposite sides of the room. Gila's rain dance had been a hit, and our team had received extra points for it. The funniest thing was that I didn't seem to care too much if I won or lost. I was having such a great time.

The comedy races began.

First, the youngest *ohel* had to run across the room, blow a ping pong ball into a cup lying on the table and then run back to the line. The girls were laughing so hard, they couldn't catch their breath long enough to blow on the ping pong ball.

The next *ohel* chosen was one of the middle groups. They had to leapfrog across the room. At first, this sounded like an easy race . . . until they were blindfolded.

Then one of the older groups had to race. Theirs was an obstacle race. Again, it sounded so simple . . . until they were told to run the obstacle course with a partner . . . with one leg of each girl tied together.

The comedy races were really hysterical, and I constantly breathed a sigh of relief that since I was a co-captain of field day, I could stand on the sidelines and watch and cheer.

I then heard the sickening announcement. Both Layah, the co-captain of Team Shemesh, and I were being called upon to run the last race. I hammed it up, making sure nobody knew how I was jittering inside. And then the instructions were given to us.

"Okay," Ruchie said. "I have two dozen raw eggs over here."

And just to demonstrate to us that they were really raw eggs, she cracked one open before our eyes. The insides of my stomach dropped to the floor.

"Now, I am going to place these eggs on the floor in a haphazard pattern. Every time you step on an egg, you . . ." she paused dramatically, "well, we all crack up."

Everyone laughed at the pun, while Layah and I groaned.

"And for each egg you miss," Ruchie continued, "you are one step ahead towards winning."

I was never so embarrassed. Here I was, a person who hates to be stared at, and now I was the center of attention. I felt so ridiculous.

"Oh, one other thing I forgot to mention," Ruchie added. "We have to blindfold you."

Great, I said to myself. Much better. Now I don't have to look everybody in the face.

As Layah and I were blindfolded, many thoughts flitted through my mind. Will they really put raw eggs out?

"Ready, set, begin."

I gingerly picked up my foot real high and placed it down again. One step, clear. I breathed a sigh of relief. Very hesitantly, I picked up my left leg and put it down carefully. Again, I was home free. I began to gain more confidence.

Suddenly, I heard everyone laughing very hard. I picked up my right foot and . . . yechhh! I couldn't believe it! They really were raw eggs. I could feel my face get red. Oh well, I'm not a quitter.

I picked up my right foot again and let it down. Nothing. I took a step with my left foot. Nothing. I heard everyone go hysterical again, and I guessed Layah had just stepped on an egg.

Oooh. What was that I had just stepped into. It didn't feel like an egg. Could it possibly have been a tub of mud? Two mud baths in one day! No wonder they had told us to take off our shoes and stockings before we began the race. It seemed they were putting more than just raw eggs in our paths.

I continued to walk on further. I picked up my foot, which was now sticky and wet and . . . yuch! What had I stepped into now? Was it pieces of confetti? And what were those cold squiggly things? Ye-e-ech! And all this is right after my delicious shower to clean off the mud.

I sensed that I was getting near the end, because my

team was really cheering me on. Just a few more steps, I thought.

Yikes! I felt someone take off my blindfold. And there I was, standing in a baby pool full of ice cubes and bubble bath. Right next to me, with as shocked a look on her face, was Layah. I took one look at her. She took one look at me. And holding hands in the little baby pool, we started to skip around, dancing and singing.

"Dance around the Torah.
Dance around the Torah.
Alef, bais, alef, bais,
and we all fall down."

At that point, Layah and I, one thought in mind, quickly flopped into the ice cold bubble bath. The camp was laughing and clapping at the same time.

Layah and I took a magnificent, dramatic bow, and sat down in our places. Boy, two unusual baths in one day. I must really be having a lot of fun.

❀ 12 ❀

CHESSED MEMORIES

Before meeting the other members of Team Geshem to continue work on the banner and theme song, I went to take a long hot shower. I found Sara waiting for me on my bed.

"Boy," she laughed as I blow-dried my hair for the second time that day. "You must be the cleanest person in Camp Rivkah."

"Probably in the whole country," I dryly added.

When my hair was finally dry and I was dressed warmly in a heavy sweatshirt, we began to walk out the door. Night had fallen, and it was dark outside.

"Listen," Sara said. "Before we go to work at our team

headquarters, let's pass by the cottage."

"That's a good idea," I said. "Although I've been kind of busy during the day, I wasn't too busy to notice that Tante hasn't been around since last night. Do you think she's home now?"

Sara did not comment, and I knew she was withholding something from me.

"Okay, Sara," I said. "Quit it. And wipe that smug smile off of your face." I mimicked our World Geography teacher Miss Grosswald.

"I know she's home," Sara replied with a laugh. "While you were taking another one of your beauty showers, I saw her car pull up."

Sara had answered my question, but she hadn't really completed the sentence.

"And . . ." I prodded.

"And she came home with a guest," Sara continued.

"Another sick old lady," I asked.

"Nope," Sara answered. "Today she came home with a different lady. This lady is not old and doesn't look sick at all."

"So what's your plan?" I asked Sara, afraid of her response.

"Well," she answered with a twinkle in her eye. "Let's do some *chessed*. Let's try to do the *mitzvah* of *bikur cholim*."

Why is it that whenever Sara wants to do something which might be interpreted as "not quite right" she veils it as a *mitzvah* or an act of *chessed*? Do I really look so naive?

"Why not?" I said with a shrug. What else could go wrong today?

We quickly walked through the night until we reached the path to Tante's cottage. It was a dark night, since the clouds had returned and insisted on hiding the moon. Every so often, the moon would peek out, allowing me to see the determined look on Sara's face. I guess she was also able to see the frightened look on mine.

We went up the stairs to Tante's porch and prepared to knock on the door.

"Shhh," a voice whispered from the side of the porch.

I nearly jumped out of my skin. I found myself shivering uncontrollably.

"I'm sorry I scared you," Tante said. "Shhh. Come and sit down on the steps."

She put her arm around me, and I began to calm down.

"I didn't mean to frighten you," Tante said softly. "I just brought a friend home from the hospital. She isn't feeling very well, and so I put her straight to bed. Is there something I can do to help you?"

"Well, the truth is," Sara said, "that we came to ask you the same question."

"Oh?"

"Well, I noticed you brought in a sick woman," Sara explained. "And we wanted to do the *mitzvah* of *bikur cholim*."

Tante took a look at the two of us. She wasn't fooled. She knew the truth. She knew we had really come to spy on her. She patted me on the knee. It was reassuring.

"Do you have time for a story?" she asked.

We both nodded.

"A really long story?" she persisted.

We nodded again.

"Well, this story begins many, many years ago," she said in a serious voice. "Oh, a little less than fifty years ago, in a place called Bergen-Belsen, a Nazi concentration camp."

As we sat on the creaky wooden steps that led to Tante's cottage, Tante transferred our thoughts and minds to a distant land and a distant time.

"My family was lucky," said Tante. "We came from a small town in Hungary. All during the early years of the war, we were able to survive in our little village. Nobody bothered us, and our Hungarian neighbors were not inter-ested in reporting us to the Nazis. My father had suc-ceeded in obtaining a passport to America for himself during the 1930's. He hoped to obtain visas for my sister and me and send for us. But then the war broke out before we were able to go to America. We lived quietly with our old grandmother, and nobody bothered us. We were sure we would be able to continue that peaceful existence until the war was over, and my father would be able to send for us once again. But the Nazis had other plans."

Tante's voice drifted off. Impatient as I was to hear the continuation of her story, I knew it was probably sad and depressing. Tante's face was shadowed, and her eyes were veiled in pain.

"The concentration camp was terrible. It was so horri-ble, I am sure my memory of it must have softened over the years."

Tante shivered.

"The physical discomforts were bad enough. We didn't have enough to eat or drink. We were always cold. The clothing we were first issued did not quite fit us, but we were told by others to accept and not complain. Our beds were wooden planks. My sister and I slept together, trying to warm each other up.

"We were both spoiled, my sister and I." Tante laughed mirthlessly. "The people in our barracks took very special care of me and my sister. They adopted us as their own. They nurtured us. They fed us. They loved us. They even played with us. They did our work for us. The last year of the war, it seems we were not watched as carefully as the other years. It was a miracle my sister and I had been saved. It was a greater miracle we survived. And it was the greatest miracle that we found ourselves among such special friends."

Tante's voice now grew stronger, and she looked at both Sara and me in turn.

"I am alive today because of the *chessed* of my room-mates," she continued. "Do you see? The Nazis tried to take everything from us. They tortured our bodies. They took away our self-esteem. They turned our self-images inside out. They tried to make us rebel against Hashem. And all the time they would sit on the sidelines, their overstuffed bodies rolling in the mire of their abuses, making fun of us. But there was one thing they were unable to take from us. Even now, forty-five years later, I can feel the pride and self-sacrifice of my neighbors. The Nazis could not change the inherent quality of being a

Torah-observant Jew. They could not take away our *midah* of *chessed*."

Tante paused. I knew she had not finished expressing her thoughts.

"My friends in the concentration camp sustained me only because of their *midah* of *chessed*. We were just little girls, ages seven and nine. It would have been easier to take our food rations for themselves. They could have found numerous excuses to do so. We were only little children who were not expected to survive. But they didn't. And why didn't they? Because of the *midah* of *chessed*. The *midah* of *chessed* and thoughtfulness and kindness was the only reason we survived.

"My sister and I were nursed through sickness. We were sheltered from the angry guards. We were protected from the harsh elements. And all through the acts of *chessed*."

Tante paused so she could emphasize her point.

"That is the reason that I helped found this camp. I am not known as one of the founders, but I was instrumental in maintaining the camp. I was also the strong voice behind the *chessed* program and the development of *midos*. Because of the *chessed* done for me in the concentration camp, I swore to be a source of *chessed* to others."

Tante wasn't telling us anything new. We knew the reputation of the camp was one of *midos tovos* and *chessed*. We also knew Tante's reputation was a personification of *chessed*. But hitting a sick woman certainly was not an act of *chessed*. Was Tante going to explain that to us? And what about the diamonds? I hesitated to pry. But I guess we didn't look too convinced, because Tante smiled and continued.

"And how am I a person of *chessed*," she questioned, reading our minds, "if I hit a woman who is down?"

Sara and I nodded our heads guiltily.

"The woman you saw is very ill," Tante continued. "I am a licensed nurse, and I take patients into my home to help them recuperate. That woman had been dismissed from the hospital prematurely. The hospital had insisted that she be released the evening you saw her with me. The trip up to the mountains was extremely difficult for her, and I had to stop many times just to give the woman an opportunity to rest. When we arrived in camp it was almost midnight."

Sara and I looked at each other. So that explained why the engine was warm that night!

"The next day, when you saw us in the kitchen," Tante was saying, "the woman was drifting in and out of consciousness, and I was trying to revive her. I was helpless, though, and she had to return to the hospital."

Tante stood up suddenly, dismissing us. Her manner abruptly changed from one of confidence to one of brisk business.

"B-b-but," Sara began, "whatever happened to your sister?"

"And what other *chessed* do you do?" I continued.

"And what about the *diamonds*?" Sara added breathlessly.

Tante curtly nodded her head at our questions, and without giving any answers, she entered her cottage and closed the door behind her.

Sara and I stood rooted to our spots.

"What a strange story," I said.

"What a strange person," Sara added, indicating Tante's closed door.

ఞ**13**ఞ

DECISIONS, DECISIONS, DECISIONS

Sara and I slowly walked toward our respective Field Day headquarters with thoughts of Tante on our minds.

When I walked into the arts and crafts building, I was shocked to see how much had been accomplished. The banner was almost finished. It was a masterpiece. A magnificent scene of peace and beauty was painted in muted colors. The whole picture seemed to be behind a misty screen, the *Gishmei Bracha*.

"Hi," Rivky greeted me. "You came just in time to review the theme song. I think that with enough practice we could be out of here by midnight."

"I am astounded," I said to Rivky and anyone else who

was willing to listen. "When did you work on the banner?"

"If you noticed," Chaya said as she completed the finishing touches with her paintbrush, "we weren't at night activity. I need my good night's sleep, so I decided to come here and work instead."

"I had already sketched out the banner," Deenie added.

"Even those of us who are not so talented," Bayla smilingly contributed, "helped paint. It was like color by number."

Again, I found Sara's words coming true. The spirit that prevailed in this Field Day was truly a team effort.

I thought about camp the previous year when I had been at Camp Danya. I had a grand time at Field Day then too. Although I had been younger and did not really participate in the planning, I did remember how my counselor cried herself to sleep one night. She was the sole artist on her team. She had talent, but no one had offered to assist her. She had stayed up all night working on the banner by herself. When she finished, the Field Day captains had unending compliments for her. When their team lost Field Day, though, the other counselors talked about my counselor behind her back. They blamed the loss of Field Day on her lack of talent. Their appreciation had been short-lived, and my counselor had suffered profusely because of it.

As I looked at our banner, I was struck by the contrast. Here, so many girls had contributed towards its completion. There wasn't one girl alone who could take the honor or the disgrace. It was truly a team effort.

We practiced and practiced the theme song. Rivky felt it

was great, but I thought something was missing. As I sang the melody for about the fiftieth time that night, it suddenly dawned on me how we could find the key to the success of the theme song. It was Aviva, whose beautiful harmony still echoed in my mind. I timidly voiced my suggestion to Rivky.

"Do you think she could do it?" she asked.

"I don't know," I answered. "But I am willing to try. If worst comes to worst and she chickens out at the last minute and doesn't want to perform, we can always go back to our original plan."

"Then you had better go to sleep right now," Rivky advised, "if you want to awaken at six o'clock in the morning and teach the harmony to Aviva."

I nodded and bid everyone good night. I knew I was taking a gamble, but I wanted to see if Aviva's cure was temporary or if she was really on the road to recovering her speech. I kept on reviewing the goals of the camp in my mind. Was I being selfish and "using" Aviva's beautiful voice to attain my selfish goal? I knew that if a little eight year old girl could perform, it would truly capture the hearts of the judges. Was Aviva's success my true concern . . . or was winning the Field Day really what I had in mind? Moreover, did I have the right to expose her to an audience? What if she wasn't ready and by my misjudgment I would mar her for life?

I went to sleep, tossing and turning, hoping that in the morning's sunlight I would be able to come to a more honest conclusion.

I looked at my watch for about the hundredth time that

night. I couldn't sleep. I don't know if I was anxious about Field Day in general or about Aviva in particular. I decided to get up, wash, get dressed and *daven* to myself. Maybe if I would sit alone and meditate I would come to the right conclusion.

I very quietly did what I planned to do, and when I finished, I sat down on the porch steps. I watched the mists rise and drift away. Soon, it would be *boker tov*, and I still had not reached a decision. I started as I saw someone approaching me out of the mists. I squinted, trying to discern her features. I felt my body tighten as I realized it was Tante coming to meet me on the steps.

"Couldn't sleep?" she inquired softly. "A lot on your mind? Decisions to make?"

I nodded. Tante sat down on the step next to me before I even had a chance to invite her. Did I really want her to sit there?

I looked away into the distance. I was very uncomfortable. I didn't know what to say to Tante, or even if it was polite to speak to her before she was ready to speak to me.

First of all, Tante was an adult. She could do whatever she pleased. Did Sara and I have a right to pry into her affairs to find out about the sick ladies, her history and those diamonds she claimed to have lost?

And what about Aviva? Sitting here on the porch steps, alone in my thoughts, I still hadn't decided what to do about Aviva.

As if Tante had a direct line to my thoughts, she began to speak.

"I told you and Sara about my life in the concentration

camp," she said, "but I didn't tell you what happened at the end of the war.

"About a month before the Allies freed us, I became very sick. I don't know if it was something I had eaten or something else. At first, I was sick to my stomach. I had such severe pains I can show you the exact spot where it hurt me, even today."

And she pointed to a spot midway between her rib cage and her stomach.

"My friends, whom I really call my *chessed* people, tried to cure me. When they saw they couldn't do that, they tried to cover up for me and shelter me. They did not want me to be sent to the hospital, for that would surely be a journey of death. But I was discovered, and they were told to prepare me for transfer to the hospital. I cried. My *chessed* people cried. My sister cried."

Tante paused in her memories.

"And then what happened?" I ventured to ask. "What happened to you? And to the *chessed* people? And to your sister?"

Tante looked first at me. Her eyes were glazed with unshed tears. She looked way off into the distance, perhaps all the way back to those days in the concentration camp. And then she looked back at me again.

"They were gone, all gone. Although the *chessed* people thought that by sending me to the hospital they were sending me to my death, ironically, that journey saved me. The camp was bombed, and only the hospital had survived. I was never able to find a trace of anyone."

We sat in silence for a few more minutes. I thought

about Tante's story. I searched for a message in her story. Why had I not been able to sleep? Why had I come out onto the porch steps? Why was Tante walking in the mists at these early hours of the morning? Why had she sat herself down to talk to me? And why did she tell me the story of her survival?

Tante slowly stood up, smoothed her skirt and touched my cheek.

"Sometimes we make decisions we think are wrong," she said. "But Hashem guides our decisions so they come out right. My *chessed* people thought it was wrong to place me in the hospital. But that action saved me. You might have doubts about your decisions. But if it is done with a true heart, you must trust in Hashem to guide your actions."

With those words, Tante glided away into the mist. At that moment, all my doubts about her sanity and sincerity were erased from my thoughts. I only saw her as a profile of *chessed* and love.

&⅚ 14 &⅚

DISCOVERING THE DIAMONDS

Aviva and I stood on the makeshift stage listening to the applause. We had just performed our theme song and introduced our banner. All my fears about Aviva turned out to be completely unfounded. She had performed like a pro. Her clear voice harmonized like a sweet bird and hypnotized the audience. We held hands tightly and walked off.

We were immediately surrounded by our teammates complimenting us. I looked at Aviva, but she wasn't frightened at all. She was smiling and enjoying the attention. I noticed Tante in the background. She nodded her approval and turned to leave.

"Come on back from dreamland," Sara nudged me. "You were great!"

I felt great, too. Just by seeing Aviva's reaction to the applause helped me realize Hashem had truly guided my decision to be the right one.

"Hey, I've got news for you," I whispered to Sara.

She pulled me off to a corner of the social hall, and I revealed to her what had happened to me with Tante that morning.

"See," Sara said. "That's the old Tante. That's the Tante everyone knows. She would always be around when a person needed her, giving advice and being right on target."

"So there really isn't any mystery about Tante," I slowly concluded.

"Oh yes, there is," Sara interrupted. "First of all, our family has been going to Camp Rivkah for a million years. Well, not quite that long. But nobody has ever known she was in a concentration camp. Or that she had a sister. Or about her *chessed* people. Why is she suddenly talking to us? Why after all these years are we learning all these intimate details of her past life?"

I wanted to defend Tante because she had helped me so much that morning, but I didn't get a chance to say anything.

"And those people," Sara rushed on. "She says she does *chessed* for those people. If she's a nurse like she claims she is, then she gets paid to do the job. That's not an act of *chessed*."

Again I tried to interrupt, but Sara wouldn't let me get

one word in. She was a locomotive running full speed ahead.

"And what about those diamonds?" she said. "We've been digging and digging and digging. We've fixed up Tante's garden beautifully, but we still haven't found any diamonds."

Finally, Sara paused long enough to let me get a word in. Unfortunately, the only thing that stuck in my mind was the question of the diamonds. And to that I had no answer.

"Yes," I agreed. "Why was Tante yelling about her diamonds?"

"Well, it's *chessed* time now," said Sara. "Let's go get Aviva and work in the garden. Maybe today will be our lucky day, and we will uncover the treasure in the garden."

Holding Aviva between us, we playfully skipped to Tante's cottage. The sun was shining brightly, and the air was very comfortable. We basked in the splendor of the beautiful summer day.

At Tante's cottage, we were greeted by two individuals.

"Hello," Tante said. "Let me introduce you to my guest Miss Gittle. Miss Gittle will be staying with me for about a week. Miss Gittle, this is Sara and this is Bracha, the two girls I have mentioned to you."

While we were being introduced, Sara and I just stood there quite formally and, at least on my part, definitely embarrassed. I wondered what terrible things Tante had "mentioned" to Miss Gittle about us, and I could see that the same thoughts had crossed Sara's mind.

"And this is little Aviva," Tante continued. "I told you how they have taken over all my gardening chores."

Sara bent her head in embarrassment, and I felt my face get red. Here we go again, I said to myself. Judging someone harshly.

"Come, Aviva," Tante said, taking her hand. "Miss Gittle has some lessons to teach Sara and Bracha. We'll work in the garden."

Aviva happily skipped to the corner of the garden, and both she and Tante began to work diligently. We watched them for a little while, and then Sara turned to Miss Gittle. She seemed bent on interrogating Miss Gittle.

"What's the matter with Tante?" Sara began her inquiry. "She isn't acting herself."

Miss Gittle let a slight smile teasingly play on her lips.

"Oh?" was her only response.

"Well, she's not acting rationally," Sara continued.

These words seemed to shock Miss Gittle.

"In what way is she acting irrationally?" she asked.

"Well, like just now," Sara said. "We are supposed to be doing our *chessed* activity. That means working in the garden. But Tante assigned us to schoolwork. She's making us listen to you." As soon as Sara said those words, she tried to retract them. "I mean, not that I wouldn't like to listen to you . . ."

As Sara's voice trailed off, I tried to save the situation.

"Sara means that we're supposed to be doing *chessed* work," I explained. "Now is not *shiur* time."

I also began to get flustered as I saw I was doing a bad job of explaining myself.

Miss Gittle sat up straight. She was a commanding presence. Although she had been sitting since we were introduced, she gave an appearance of someone who was very tall. As she looked us over, I felt myself cringing.

"Sometimes *chessed* involves acts of kindness done to another person," said Miss Gittle, her soft voice belying her personage. "And sometimes it is an act of *chessed* simply to tolerate someone else."

Sara and I exchanged looks. There was a lesson Miss Gittle was trying to convey to us. Were we being intolerant of Tante?

"But this year," Sara explained, "she sometimes does things that are uncharacteristic of her as we know her from previous years."

Miss Gittle raised her eyebrows. But the words she said were not critical of us.

"Maybe you didn't know the real Tante," she said.

"And who is the real Tante?" I asked, remembering the sweet advice of this morning and the demented gardener of a few weeks before.

Miss Gittle looked at us and then shifted her gaze to where Tante was diligently working on her garden, assisted by Aviva.

"Let me tell you about myself," Miss Gittle said, "and then you will understand Tante and her acts of *chessed* a little better.

"I am a very sick woman."

We both sat up straighter.

"Oh no," Miss Gittle said, and softly laughed. "I am not telling you this because I want pity. As a matter of fact, it is because nobody knows how sick I am that I have come to know and to love Tante.

"I have a dreaded disease. My disease has no cure. When it was discovered I was ill, the doctors told me I had only five months to live. That was five and a half years ago."

Miss Gittle paused as we digested this information.

"When I was told by the doctors I was going to die, I at first began to cry. I thought of my two children and my husband. I thought of my elderly parents. How was I ever going to be able to reveal to these people the definitive verdict my doctors had proclaimed?

"I cried. I found out on *Shabbos*, and I cried the whole *Shabbos*. On Sunday morning, my husband came in to visit me. That Sunday we both cried all day. At the end of the day, though, my husband and I reached a conclusion. We had decided that although my doctors did not think I would live beyond *Pesach*, I would fight this illness."

Miss Gittle paused.

"Sometimes people fight a disease by attacking," she went on. "They announce to the world that they are ill and that they are not going to let the disease conquer them. They enlist the aid of everyone around them. Sometimes they win.

"I'm a different personality. Never, in my whole life, have I attacked anyone or anything. I am always too shy to ask for help. I am very quiet and reserved. Because of the nature of my personality, my husband and I decided to wage a war against my disease in the manner befitting my personality. I would not let anyone other than my husband and my two children know I was terminally ill. If I could fool the world into thinking I was a healthy person, then I would be able to conquer my disease."

I was not quite sure I understood what Miss Gittle was saying, but I need not have worried. Sara voiced my question.

"But weren't you just fooling yourself?" she asked. "Can't people see you are very ill? And how does that help you fight the disease?"

"As I have said, I've been ill for five and a half years," Miss Gittle answered. "My parents still don't know. And how does it help me fight the disease? If I give in to my pain and I cry in public, I will be relieved from the burden of that moment of pain. But if I can hide my pain for that moment, until I can be alone, I have then been able to gather my strength for the next attack. It's like a war. My illness is my enemy. If I can subdue my enemy by not admitting defeat and crying out in pain, then I can gather my troops to fight my enemy when the battle is harder."

I looked at Miss Gittle in awe.

"You're a remarkable person," I said.

"Oh, but I'm not," Miss Gittle protested. "Tante is the remarkable person. Every time I receive my medication for my disease I am in a great deal of pain. I find that at that time I don't have the emotional strength to face my family, never mind the rest of the world. I am too weak to pretend I am well. I am not ill enough to stay in the hospital, but I am in too much pain to go home. That is when I visit Tante. She is the only one outside my immediate family who knows I am sick. She is my pillar of strength. She makes sure I don't fall. She gives me the *mussar* I need and helps me draw my strength by saying *Tehillim* with me."

Miss Gittle stood up. She was extremely tall, almost six feet. But her walk was very delicate. She turned to face us when she reached the doorway and held on to the posts for support.

"I'm really not feeling too well now," she said. "That is a reaction to my medication. For the next two days, I might say things to you that may seem strange. It will be the combination of medication coupled with unusual pain. Don't be frightened. I will pull off what my doctors now call another miracle. One other thing, though. Tante doesn't know I am speaking to you about her. There are lessons of *emunah* and *bitachon* she wanted me to discuss with you. I'll have to discuss that with you at a later time. Just remember to cherish your Tante. She is a gem. And her acts of kindness are like diamonds."

Tante noticed that Miss Gittle had gone back into the cottage, and she hurriedly dropped what she was doing and followed Miss Gittle inside. Aviva slowly followed her to the steps and clasped our hands. Although the sun was shining, we felt a new chill in the air. It was a forewarning of the battle Miss Gittle was about to wage.

"Come on, General," Sara said to Aviva, mocking a marching step. "We're off to lunch!"

I didn't follow. I was still stunned by the words Miss Gittle had just spoken.

"What's with you?" Sara asked. "Aren't you coming?"

I nodded and slowly followed.

"She's a gem," I repeated. "And her acts of kindness are diamonds."

❧ **15** ❧

UNEXPECTED ANSWERS

I repeated the words again.

"Do you think the diamonds Tante was screaming about were her acts of *chessed*?" I asked.

Sara thoughtfully stood rooted to the spot.

"But why the garden?" she said. "What do the flowers and vegetables in the garden have to do with *chessed*? If Tante means her acts of *chessed* are her diamonds, then why did she refer to her garden and cry about the ruins of the garden?"

Sara seemed doubtful about my theory. I myself was beginning to believe it was just a theory and not an actual interpretation. But we had questioned Miss Gittle about

Tante's claim of lost diamonds, and Miss Gittle concluded her discussion with us by making a point of referring to Tante's acts of *chessed* as diamonds.

Sara shrugged her shoulders.

"This is getting much too complicated for me to understand right now," she said. "Anyhow, we've got to wash up and get to lunch. I can't wait for the marathon race this afternoon."

We slowly but purposefully led Aviva back to her *ohel*, discussing Tante's strange behavior while we walked. As we walked and talked, Aviva began humming a tune under her breath.

"That's beautiful, Aviva," I said. And though not really expecting any response, I then asked her. "Where did you learn that lovely lullaby, Aviva? It does sound like a lullaby, doesn't it, Sara?"

Ever since we had begun working with Aviva, Sara and I always included her in our conversations. Sometimes, we would even ask her questions, hoping for a response but never getting one. We eventually just got into the habit of asking Aviva a question and then quickly either responding ourselves or continuing our conversation with another topic.

"Tante," Aviva answered.

I continued walking, not quite comprehending what had just happened.

"What did you say?" I asked Aviva, just like I would ask any other normal eight-year-old if I hadn't heard her answer.

"Tante," Aviva repeated.

Sara and I stopped walking and then immediately continued our journey. I felt my hands begin to shake and my heart do acrobatics. I tried to act calmly and in my usual manner.

"Oh," I repeated to make sure I wasn't hearing things. "Did Tante teach you that tune?"

Aviva nodded her head, seemingly oblivious to the wild shenanigans she was causing in my emotions.

"When did Tante teach you the tune?" Sara continued to question Aviva, quite calmly, but I was able to detect the excitement in her voice.

"Today," Aviva answered. "When you were talking with Miss Gittle."

We tried to remain calm, but it wasn't easy. I silently told my racing heart to slow down. We had reached Aviva's *ohel*, and I gave her my usual hug and kiss and waved her on her way.

"See you later," Aviva said, repeating Sara's usual farewell.

My head was dizzy, and my palms were sweaty. I shivered.

"She spoke," I said to Sara.

"Yes," Sara repeated in as an astounded voice as mine. "She spoke. Whoopie!"

"I can't believe it!" I said in a jubilant voice.

We were so excited that we sang and danced and laughed our way to our *ohel*.

"Binny! Binny!" I cried when I saw Aviva's cousin.

"You'll never believe it," Sara added.

I tried to remain calm, but I couldn't.

"Sit down before I faint," I said.

"What?" said Binny

"I mean," I repeated flustered and in quite a mixed up fashion, "sit down before *you* faint!"

"Why should I faint?" Binny asked, looking at the two of us uncomprehendingly. "What is going on? What are you two talking about?"

I wanted to confess the news in a calmer attitude, but Sara was having none of that nonsense.

"Hooray! Hooray! Hooray!" Sara cried. "Aviva talked. Aviva talked!"

Binny stood frozen to the spot. She looked at us in bewilderment.

"What did you say?" she asked, afraid that we were teasing her.

I repeated what Sara had said.

"It's true, Binny," I said. "We were having a normal conversation with Aviva, like we always do. We asked her a question, not expecting an answer."

"We're always asking her questions," Sara interrupted. "We never expect her to answer our questions, but we feel she's so much a part of our conversations we always ask her questions."

"Only this time," I concluded the story, "only this time, Aviva did answer us."

We then related the whole conversation to Binny. We were so excited that we just kept on interrupting each other. Binny sat with her mouth open in awe as we repeated the events of the morning. Finally, Binny stood up.

"I'm going to call my mother right now," Binny declared. "She'll know what to do. I'm so excited! I just can't believe it."

Neither could we. With bouncing spirits we washed up for lunch and entered the dining room.

❀ 16 ❀

A MARATHON OF SKILL

Around twenty girls took part in the marathon race. We were standing at the starting line listening to the instructions Ruchie was explaining to us.

"Never let the baton leave your hand," she repeated, "until you are sure the girl who is to run the next lap is ready to receive it. I have seen marathons lost because of the hastiness of one team which caused the baton to be dropped numerous times."

There was so much to remember. I carried the list with each team member's part in my hands. Seventy-five points depended on this marathon.

"Good luck," Sara called from her team's side of the

basketball court. "Enjoy the races!"

"Good luck," I called back.

I was finally getting in the spirit of Camp Rivkah. It really didn't matter if you won or lost, as long as you were having fun.

"On your marks," Ruchie said.

Zeesy stood at our team's line, jumping up and down and ready to go.

"Get ready," Ruchie said.

Zeesy flashed us all a sign of victory.

"Oh, by the way," Ruchie conversationally interrupted the race. "Did you hear the joke about . . .?"

She was greeted with moans and groans from the crowd. I looked around in puzzlement.

"Ruchie is known for the way she tries to stretch out the starting of a race," Rivky explained to me.

"Oh, you heard that one already," Ruchie continued.

She was greeted with verbal rotten tomatoes.

"Okay," she sighed. "Let's start again."

"On your marks," Ruchie began again.

"Get ready," Ruchie said for the second time.

"One second, Zeesy," Ruchie again halted the count. "Didn't you forget to take your medication?"

"Ruchie!" everyone screamed.

"Okay, okay," she said. "I got the message."

"On your marks," Ruchie said for the third time. "Get ready."

This time everyone was ready to begin, even Ruchie.

"A-a-a-and . . . Go!" she shouted.

Zeesy and Shoshie began running towards the baskets

at opposite ends of the basketball court. They had to throw the ball into the baskets from the foul line. They would have five chances and would receive two points for each basket they made. As the ball fell through the net, it was greeted by cheers. If Zeesy or Shoshie missed making a basket, their teammates groaned in response. They then thrust the baton into the waiting hands of their teammates who continued the race.

The next stop was the computer room. Debbie and Shayndy were to play a computer game. The girl who would have the highest score would gain ten points for her team.

The marathon race continued. The teams were running all over the Camp Rivkah grounds. They passed the baton from the girl in the computer room to the girl down by the pool. She had to dive for coins. The total value of the coins retrieved were then added to the score.

Then it was back to the front of the main building where the marathoner had to sit on balloons and burst them. Each balloon was worth another point.

The races continued, and I kept on running around, trying to add up the score along with the judges. The marathon race took the girls from one extreme end of the camp to the other. I felt the calories dripping away.

Finally, the marathon race was completed. I flopped down on the lawn in front of the main building.

"You look exhausted," I heard Sara's comment from the distance.

"I *am* exhausted," I answered. "I think I was just sleeping. Have you been standing around here long?"

"For ages," Sara answered. "About five seconds worth."

I smiled at Sara. She always had a way with words.

"While you were running around trying to win this marathon race, Binny called her mother."

"Did she get through?" I asked anxiously. "What did her mother say?"

"It took such a long time for Binny to get a full report," Sara said, "because Binny had to speak to her mother who had to speak to Aviva's mother who had to speak to Aviva's psychiatrist. Did you know Aviva was seeing a child psychiatrist?"

I shook my head.

"Then Aviva's mother called the camp," Sara continued. "And then she called Binny's mother who finally called Binny to tell her the news."

"And what is the news you are cleverly hiding?" I impatiently asked Sara.

"Aviva's parents are coming for *Shabbos*," Sara answered. "That gives us two days to prepare."

"Two days to prepare what?" I cautiously asked Sara. I was not too sure of Sara's complicated plans. "And you still haven't told me what the psychiatrist had to say."

"Well, last things first," Sara answered with a sigh. "The psychiatrist Aviva has been going to felt that Aviva has to be handled very delicately. We have to call him before we do anything."

"And so what is your plan?" I asked with just a little trepidation.

Sara whispered it into my ear.

"It'll be kind of hard," I doubtfully agreed. "Are you sure Aviva will follow through?"

"Well, I hope so," Sara admitted. "And by the way, we have a telephone appointment with Aviva's psychiatrist in about ten minutes. We are to go to the director's office to await the phone call."

❧ **17** ❧

THE PSYCHIATRIC ANGLE

Sara sat on one hard wooden chair, while I sat on the other. Rabbi Rubin's office was overflowing with papers. The secretary and the bookkeeper were shifting papers and files around.

"Excuse me," the secretary said as she almost dropped a folder of medical reports on my head.

Her pencil was sticking out behind her ear, and her glasses kept slipping down to the point of her nose. Sara and I exchanged glances. We could hardly keep from giggling. The secretary looked like a female absent-minded professor.

The telephone rang insistently. Each time the bell rang,

I jumped and began getting nervous all over again. I wished we had already completed our talk with the psychiatrist. Finally, the telephone rang, and Rabbi Rubin ushered everyone else out of the room. This was the phone call we had been waiting for. Rabbi Rubin handed two extensions to us and left the room, closing the door quietly behind him.

Peace at last.

"Hello," said the voice on the telephone. "Dr. Elliot speaking."

"Hello, my name is Sara Goodman."

"And I am Bracha Friedman," I added as Sara nudged me.

"We would like to discuss the case of Aviva Miller," Sara explained. "I don't know if you were given any background information, but both Bracha and I have been working with Aviva during the summer."

"It's all right, girls," Dr. Elliot responded. "I do have all that information in the files. How can I be of assistance to you?"

"Well," Sara continued. "Aviva spoke to us today."

Sara waited to hear Dr. Elliot's reaction to this news.

"Yes," he said.

"Well, we have a plan that involves Aviva and her parents," Sara hesitantly continued to explain. "Specifically her mother."

"Yes," said Dr. Elliot.

I saw Sara was very disturbed by the monosyllables Dr. Elliot was using for answers. I interrupted.

"We love Aviva," I said. "And we don't want to do

anything that might harm her. And we are worried that our plan might be harmful."

"And what is your plan?" Dr. Elliot asked.

"Aviva learned a beautiful tune," Sara explained. "We would like to write words to fit the tune and have Aviva sing the song for her mother this Friday night."

There was a pause while we held our breath.

"Will she sing this song in front of the whole camp?" Dr. Elliot asked. "Or just among a few people?"

Dr. Elliot's question surprised us.

"We haven't really thought about that angle," I confessed.

"Let me understand this correctly," Dr. Elliot said as he reviewed the facts. "Aviva did not speak or sing when you first came to camp?"

We nodded our heads but then realized that Dr. Elliot couldn't see us.

"Yes," I answered.

"Then after approximately a month's time Aviva harmonized a song in private with just the two of you attending?"

"Yes."

"The next step, rather a quick one I might recall, was Aviva performing a harmony in public?"

Again we agreed, this time a little sheepishly.

"Now, just a short while later, she spoke to you?"

We were getting the impression Dr. Elliot did not approve of what we had done.

"This is all very interesting," Dr. Elliot continued. "Aviva is using music as her vehicle for communicating. She loves you, so she tests out her communication with you first. She is reassured immediately, and then feels secure enough to perform in public. H·m·m·m."

I was afraid to interrupt.

"I would suggest" Dr. Elliot concluded, "to teach her the song with words. When you are certain she can perform it in public, without any mistakes, just ask her."

"Ask her?" Sara questioned.

"Ask her?" I echoed.

"Sure, just ask her," Dr. Elliot responded with a laugh. "She feels very secure with you. She has chosen to speak to the two of you. If she doesn't want to perform in public, she will tell you. Explain to her that it is a surprise for her mother."

"Oh," Sara and I answered in wonderment at the simplicity of the situation.

"And, girls," Dr. Elliot said before he hung up. "Just remember we are all just instruments of Hashem. I have been working with Aviva for over two years. Hashem did not feel I was the instrument to help achieve the miracle. Hashem chose you two girls instead. *Hatzlachah*, and have a *gutten Shabbos*."

Dr. Elliot hung up the phone. Sara and I remained in the same frozen positions, our hands still holding the telephone to our ears.

"Hey, he's Jewish!" Sara exclaimed.

"He's *frum*," I added.

"I didn't know there was such a thing as *frum* psychiatrists," I concluded by way of explanation.

"Well, that's the only kind of person who could readily

understand Aviva's background and Aviva's miracle," Sara said.

"We are all instruments of Hashem," I repeated. "He's right, you know."

"Yeah," Sara agreed. "We didn't cause Aviva to speak. Hashem did. I guess we're kind of lucky to merit being there when the miracle actually occurred."

❧ **18** ❧

THE EVERYDAY MIRACLES

Sara and I slowly walked back to our *ohel.*

"Let's stop by Tante's on the way back to our bunk," Sara suggested. "Maybe we'll get a chance to see and to speak to Miss Gittle. She is such an interesting person, and besides, we can to do the *mitzvah* of *bikur cholim.*"

I laughed quietly to myself. But I couldn't fool Sara. She noticed I was smiling, and she smiled in response. We both knew that in order to pass by Tante's cottage we would have to make a long detour; it was not just on the way. But our curiosity was too strong.

As we emerged from under the trees, we saw Tante weeding her garden. She was dressed in the same outfit she had worn on the night of the counselor's hunt. I didn't understand. We had seen Tante gardening on numerous occasions since that first time, but we had never seen her in that outlandish outfit since then. I exchanged glances with Sara. She just shrugged and ventured forth. Tante was humming the same tune Aviva had been humming this morning.

"Hi," we greeted her.

Tante's thoughts were focused elsewhere, and it took a few moments until she realized we were there.

"Hi," Sara repeated a little more loudly.

Tante shivered and then looked at us.

"Sorry, girls," she said. "Sometimes I get in my moods, and I forget where I am." She paused. "I was remembering my *chessed* people."

I saw Sara did not quite understand what was happening. Neither did I. Would Sara, in her outspoken way, demand an explanation?

Then Tante seemed to realize what she was wearing. She looked down at her clothes.

"Oh, excuse my appearance," she said quite sedately. "When I plan on working in my garden for a few hours, I usually wear what I call my gardening uniform. That way I won't dirty my dress."

"Oh," Sara and I answered quietly. It was a such a simple explanation.

"Let me help you," I said to Tante as she began to gather her gardening tools together.

As Sara took the bulk of the equipment, I reached out to carry the numerous vegetables and flowers Tante had just picked from her garden.

"Oh no you don't," Tante playfully slapped my hand. "You can help me with all my equipment," Tante paused dramatically, "but only I get to carry my diamonds."

"Your diamonds?" Sara and I repeated uncomprehendingly.

"That's right," Tante said. "These fresh flowers and vegetables are the fruits of my labor. They are my diamonds. They help me demonstrate real acts of *chessed*."

"I don't understand," I mumbled.

"Oh yes you do," Tante teased. "Don't you think I figured out why two young AJCs wanted to help me in my garden? Especially one young lady who can't stand gardening?"

Tante looked directly at Sara.

"Well, I like to garden now," Sara feebly suggested.

"I knew all along that your excuse for gardening was really so you could search for my hidden diamonds," Tante said.

I blushed outrageously.

"Little did you know you would be instrumental in producing the diamonds," Tante added.

I still didn't quite understand.

"Every day, I take some flowers, fruits and vegetables to the local hospital," Tante explained. "Every Tuesday and Thursday, I also take some to the nursing home. Patients receive adequate care and food in these institutions, but when I come laden with my special home-grown variety, the patients are extremely appreciative. It helps them get better quicker, because they know someone went out of their way to do something exclusively for their pleasure. That's why I call the food I grow in my garden diamonds. These diamonds help me create sparkling acts of *chessed*. Like sparkling diamonds."

I was left without an answer. Here we had devoted our whole summer to solving the mystery of the buried diamonds, only to find out there weren't any real diamonds at all. And Miss Gittle *had* been right. Tante's diamonds were really her acts of *chessed*.

"I see you're disappointed," Tante teased.

"Well," Sara sheepishly admitted. "I kind of really had my hopes up there were real diamonds buried in the garden."

"Yes," Tante agreed. "But *these* diamonds are definitely more precious."

We nodded in agreement.

"I don't want to change the subject," Tante interrupted, "but Miss Gittle asked that you visit her next time you came by. Come with me."

We nodded again, anxious to meet with Miss Gittle another time. Tante stopped as we reached the foot of the stairs to the porch.

"I feel I must prepare you," she said. "Miss Gittle does not look well. At times, she may start a sentence and not complete it. Don't feel you have to respond to what she says. Miss Gittle wants to give you a message of *bitachon*."

Tante took us both by the hands and led us into her cottage.

I had just a fleeting glance of the neat kitchen before

Tante led us into one of the bedrooms.

The room was bright and airy, unlike the typical camp cottages. The walls were painted a bright yellow color that enveloped the room with sun and warmth. Miss Gittle was lying on a hospital bed in the middle of the room. Next to her bed were numerous bottles of medication. There were cabinets and tables neatly arranged with medical equipment. There was a portable oxygen tank in the corner of the room.

Miss Gittle indicated two chairs near her bed.

"Please sit," she said in a hoarse voice.

Sara and I gingerly sat on the edge of the wooden chairs. Tante took her place behind us. We waited for Miss Gittle to speak.

"Now that I have you sitting here in front of me," she said, "I don't know how to begin."

We didn't answer. She laughed and then coughed.

"I'm in a lot of pain," Miss Gittle said.

We nodded and waited.

"Dovid Hamelech says that all of his bones *daven* to Hashem. When I am in so much pain and there isn't one spot in my body that doesn't hurt me, I understand completely what Dovid Hamelech meant."

We listened silently.

"Do you ever say *Tehillim*?"

Again, we nodded our heads.

"Of course you say *Tehillim*," Miss Gittle corrected herself. "I'm sure you say a couple of *kapitlach Tehillim* every day. But do you *really* say *Tehillim*? Do you understand what you are saying?

"Before I got sick, I said *Tehillim*. But now I understand *Tehillim* so much better. There are *kapitlach* written for every single emotion I have. *Tehillim* saves me. Dovid Hamelech went through every single experience possible and survived. Saying *Tehillim* makes me realize I can reach the depths of despair, yet Hashem will support me and bring me up once again."

Miss Gittle paused, and I thought she was finished speaking. Then her voice continued.

"If Dovid Hamelech could survive, then so can I," Miss Gittle continued. "Sometimes I think Hashem is testing me with the pain of this disease. 'Well,' I say to Hashem. 'You can stop testing me, because I will never give up the hope and *bitachon* that You will send me a *refuah she-laymah.*' "

It seemed Miss Gittle was finished. Her eyes were closed, and she was breathing heavily. We looked at Tante, but she just shook her head. Miss Gittle still wanted to talk with us.

"There's one more thing I'd like to tell you," Miss Gittle said. "I told you yesterday that when I was diagnosed the doctors gave me five months to live. I have survived for over five years. That is against their statistics. Every crisis I encounter, the doctors quote statistics to me. Only one percent survive, they frequently tell me. But statistics are just numbers. Each person is an individual, and that raises him above and beyond the statistics. Hashem does not look at statistics or numbers. Hashem looks at the individual's deeds.

"Every time I reach a crisis, the doctors tell me they

doubt I will survive. But I have survived."

Miss Gittle paused to take a deep breath.

"For five years I have survived," she continued in her quiet tone of voice. "The doctors call it a miracle. But living and breathing and eating and walking are all miracles. You have seen the miracle of speech with your Aviva, as Tante told me.

"Doctors don't have control over miracles. Our daily existence is a miracle. It's just that as long as things go well, we take these everyday miracles for granted. We don't even realize that they are miracles. When you live a crisis existence like I do, you value the everyday miracle of life. So statistics don't mean anything. Illness does not mean anything. Because every breath we take is a miraculous gift from Hashem."

Miss Gittle paused and she seemed to relax. She stared at us intently.

"I'm not trying to frighten you. Sickness does exist. But Hashem, the *Rofeh Cholim*, the Supreme Doctor, has given me the gift of life for so many extra years. I believe He granted me these extra years so that I should help teach *emunah* and *bitachon* to others. Hashem wants me to help others.

"I believe I can be cured completely. I believe in that everyday miracle. Stop and think sometimes during your day. You will also thank Hashem for your miracle."

Miss Gittle's voice trailed off, and her breathing lapsed into a steady relaxed sleep. Tante softly indicated that it was time for us to leave. We tiptoed out of the room.

Thoughts of Miss Gittle's *bitachon* swirled through my

mind as I stepped down the porch steps. I thought of her miracle. I thought of Aviva's miracle. I then thought of the miracle of life itself.

"What is our purpose in life?" Sara paraphrased. "It is only to do the *mitzvos* of Hashem."

❦ **19** ❦

AND THE WINNER IS

We went back to our *ohel* in a somber mood. Miss Gittle's words echoed through my mind. Every day of life was a miracle. I looked at the green leaves on the trees and the deep blue of the sky. *Baruch Hashem*, I had the gift of sight. I smelled the perfume of the flowers and listened to the sounds of the children laughing and singing.

"There is so much I take for granted," Sara said.

Her words just verbalized my thoughts.

"I know what you mean," I agreed. "It's not that we don't care about the sad things that happen. It's just that we take the good things as if they're coming to us."

"I guess it's important for everyone to know a person

like Miss Gittle," Sara said.

"I'll tell you one thing," I said. "As the weeks go by, the reality of what Miss Gittle said will probably fall to the side and won't seem like it is so important. I'm sure I'll still go around expecting the normal miracle of my day to day existence to continue."

I paused and Sara waited for me to complete my thoughts.

"But I know for sure," I concluded, "that whenever I say *Tehillim*, I will think into the words I am saying."

Sara nodded.

"And perhaps," she said, "if I remember, I will think of how Miss Gittle interprets the *kapitlach*."

"It would be so good if Miss Gittle's lessons can be taught to everyone," I concluded thoughtfully.

Suddenly, Sara stopped short.

"Hey, maybe they could be," she said with excitement, her eyes glistening.

I didn't like the gleam in Sara's eyes.

"Come on," I said. "You saw how hard it was for Miss Gittle to express herself to us. You don't expect her to speak before the whole camp, do you?"

"No, of course not," Sara replied. "No, my idea is completely different."

I waited patiently for Sara to divulge her idea.

"Have you given any thought as to the words we will use for the song Aviva is to sing Friday night?" Sara asked.

"I kind of just thought we would play around with the meaning of *Ayshes Chayil* or something like that," I answered.

"Well, why don't we do something better?" Sara suggested. "Why don't we write a song of *bitachon* and miracles?"

I let Sara's suggestion sink in. It was a good idea, but I just didn't think I was capable of writing thoughts that would completely describe Miss Gittle's feelings. Sara saw the doubtful look on my face.

"Come on," she said. "At least say you'll try. I'll help you."

I gave in. I really did not expect to be successful, but . . . oh, well.

"All right, I'll try," I said. "But you must help me. I know I can't do it alone."

Sara's step was lighter as we walked to the dining room. Mine just dragged. I really didn't feel myself equal to the task.

After supper, we got permission from Binny to work in the seclusion of the sewing room. Sara and I both sat down with pencil and paper.

"Okay, let's go," Sara said.

"It's not so easy," I answered. "I just can't write a poem on command."

"I know how I can help you," Sara said.

Sitting in the quiet of the sewing room, Sara began to hum the tune Tante had taught Aviva.

I began to write.

Once I started, I saw that the words and thoughts kept on flowing. I erased and crossed out a little here and a little there. After a long time, the song began to take shape.

"Done," I finally said.

Sara stretched.

"Okay, let's hear it," she said.

I sang the song softly to her. It was a conglomeration of all the lessons we were taught that summer. It was a thank you to all the people who had an influence on us.

"That's great!" Sara exclaimed.

"Now I have to thank Hashem for the miracle of giving me the talent to write this song." I sighed and laughed in relief.

"*Lailah tov*, Machaneh Rivkah," we suddenly heard. "*Lailah tov.*"

"Hey, is that Ruchie on the microphone?" I asked.

"It sure sounds like her," Sara answered. "Shhh."

"I'm sure you're all tired from running around during Field Day," Ruchie continued speaking on the microphone. "You're really not interested in hearing who won, right?"

Sara and I ran out to the porch of the sewing room. All the porches in the camp were overflowing with excited children and staff members waiting to see who would be announced as the winners of Field Day.

"Well," Ruchie continued. "I have the scores right here. Oh, I had them a couple of minutes ago, but I can't seem to find them now. I guess I'll tell you the winners tomorrow. *Lailah tov.*"

"Does she always do this?" I whispered to Sara.

Sara nodded.

"Well, look at what I just found," Ruchie continued, sounding surprised. "The winning team, which was Team Chalav, had 1473 points."

"Team Chalav?" I whispered to Sara. "The field day teams were Geshem and Shemesh."

"She's just teasing us," Sara answered. "Team Chalav was last year's field day team."

"O-o-oops, sorry about that," Ruchie apologized. "The truth is I wanted you to realize that although we all have to try our best to win, in the end, whether you won or lost Field Day, everyone is really a winner . . ."

I felt myself nodding.

". . . as long as you had fun. So-o-o-o the winning team is . . . Team Geshem!"

"Hooray," I said. Then I looked at Sara. "Oh, I'm sorry you lost."

Sara just shrugged her shoulders nonchalantly.

"Somebody's got to win and somebody's got to lose," she said. "Big deal."

"You're right," I agreed. "But I'm still happy my team won. Now let me practice that song one more time, and make sure we really like it. Tomorrow is *Erev Shabbos*, and we don't have that much time to teach the song to Aviva."

&20&

THE SONG OF FAITH

The *Shabbos Seudah* was finished. *Shabbos* at Camp Rivkah was always a very special time. The atmosphere was festive. Every girl was dressed in her *Shabbos* best. Gone were the sneakers of the weekday activities. Gone were the paint-streaked smocks and the mismatched outfits. When Camp Rivkah welcomed the *Shabbos*, the whole camp sparkled with a special shine ... like Tante's *chessed* diamonds.

I looked around the room as Ruchie prepared to make her announcement and introduce Aviva's song. I was sitting with Sara right in the front, in case Aviva would need us. Aviva's parents were sitting at the head table, a little to the left of where Aviva would be standing. Mrs. Miller had heard Aviva speak, but she had not been told of the surprise song.

I continued looking around the room and saw Tante sitting a little way from the head table, kind of in the background. I had hoped Miss Gittle would be with her, but I guess she wasn't feeling too well.

"We have a special treat tonight," Ruchie was saying to an absolutely quiet dining room. "Aviva Miller is going to treat us with a song that was written by Bracha Friedman."

I felt myself blushing and looked at Sara.

"I told her not to say I wrote the song," I mumbled.

Sara just smiled, so I knew she was the one who had emphasized I must be given credit for being the author. One of these days . . . I couldn't finish my thought, because Aviva then began to sing the words I had written with Tante and Miss Gittle in mind.

"In a small and lovely village
Not so many years ago
A little girl was growing older
Oblivious to the glow
Of the distant war coming closer
Bearing misery as its gift
And it tore this girl asunder
And sent her soul adrift.

But she still had her *emunah*
Her *bitachon* was so strong
It kept her spirits going

It showed her right from wrong
There are people who are suffering
Whose pain we can't explain
They value every moment
They surely don't complain
There's a lesson that they teach us
That we must value every day
It is the miracle of our existence
That's the gift that comes our way.

Yes, these people have *emunah*
Their *bitachon* is so strong
It's what keeps their spirits going
It shows them right from wrong."

I was elated. Aviva had done it. She was able to sing in public. She hadn't hesitated and she hadn't seemed insecure. Everyone was cheering, as Sara and I helped Aviva jump down from her chair, her makeshift stage.

"You were super," I reassured Aviva as she looked to me for approval.

I looked towards Mrs. Miller, anxious to see her response to Aviva's performance.

"Mommy," I heard Aviva's voice saying softly. "Why are you crying?"

Mrs. Miller was indeed crying. I exchanged looks with Sara.

"Tears of happiness," Sara said softly.

Mrs. Miller bowed down and hugged Aviva.

"That was beautiful, sweetheart," she said as she smiled

through the tears. "But who is Bracha Friedman, the girl who wrote the song?"

"I am Bracha Friedman," I quietly responded, taking a few steps forward.

The rest of the camp was being dismissed. The noise was dreadfully loud, and I couldn't wait to get out of the dining room myself. Sara took my hand for support.

"I am Bracha Friedman," I repeated.

"That song was really beautiful," Mrs. Miller began. "Where did you learn it?"

I couldn't understand her question. Did she doubt I wrote the song myself?

"I wrote it," I answered.

"I know you wrote the words," Mrs. Miller continued. "But where did you learn the tune?"

"Oh," I said. "From Tante."

"Tante?" Mrs. Miller repeated.

"Yes," I said. "Tante."

I pointed to where Tante was standing not far from our small group. Mrs. Miller searched Tante's face.

"And where did you learn the tune?" she questioned Tante softly in that same unsteady voice. Tante acted as if something powerful was happening in the dining room. I felt myself following the conversation very carefully.

"It's an old lullaby," Tante answered. "My Bubby used to sing it to my sister and me back in Europe before the war."

Tante's answer was met with absolute silence. Nobody said anything and nobody moved. Suddenly, Mrs. Miller got up from her chair. She searched Tante's face for some sign, some feature. But she said only one word.

"Bayla," she said. "Bayla?"

Tante held onto a chair for support.

"Goldie," she said softly. "Is it you? Is it really you?"

We all stood in the same positions, stunned. Binny's Aunt Goldie and our beloved Tante were really sisters! Could it be? All these years they had lived in different cities, pursuing different lifestyles, and each one did not know the other one was still alive.

The two of them were quietly crying and reminiscing. They were trying to catch up on forty-five years of their lives. Aviva walked over to us. She was just as astounded as we were.

"Can you believe it?" I questioned Aviva. "You just got a new aunt. Tante."

Aviva giggled.

"Should I call her Tante Tante?" she asked.

We all laughed at the ridiculousness of it. Our mood was so euphoric.

"You really see *Hashgachas Hashem* in this," Sara stated.

"Definitely," I agreed. "Remember when you said how all the years you were in Camp Rivkah you always took Tante for granted?"

Sara nodded.

"And how you never knew her background?"

"I couldn't understand why she was telling us her history and about the concentration camp," she said. "If you would've asked me at the beginning of camp if I would get to know Tante so intimately, I would've scoffed at the suggestion."

"And yet," I thoughtfully added, "it was because of our constant contact with her that she taught that song to Aviva."

"And that song was what brought Mrs. Miller and Tante back together . . ." said Sara

". . . after all these years," I finished the sentence for her.

I had learned a lot at Camp Rivkah that summer. So many unpredictable events had taken place. I had met so many unusual people who had made a strong impression on my life.

I looked at Sara. Life was always so exciting when Sara was around. I wondered what other exciting adventures we would encounter as the Girls of Rivkah Gross Academy High.

GLOSSARY

alef: Hebrew letter
Ayshes Chayil: Woman of Valor
b'ezras Hashem: with G-d's help
bais: house
Baruch Hashem: thank G-d
bentch: say Grace after Meals
bikur cholim: visiting the sick
bitachon: trust
bli ayin hora: with no evil eye
Bnei Yisrael: Jewish people
Bnos Yisrael: Jewish girls
boker tov: good morning
chessed: kindness
chinuch: education
daven: pray
emunah: faith
Erev Shabbos: day before the Sabbath
frum: observant
geshem: rain
Gishmei Bracha: blessed rains
gutten Shabbos: a good Sabbath
Halachah: Jewish law
Hashgachas Hashem: divine providence
Hatzlachah: good luck
kapitlach: chapters
kof: Hebrew letter

lailah tov: good night
lamed: Hebrew letter
machaneh: camp
Mashiach: Messiah
midah keneged midah: measure for measure
midos tovos: good character
Minchah: afternoon service
mitzvah: Torah commandment
mussar: ethics
neigel vasser: water for washing hands
ness: miracle
ohel: camp bunk
Pesach: Passover
refuah shelaymah: full recovery
Rofeh Cholim: the Supreme Doctor
sefer: book
Shabbos Seudah: Sabbath meal
Shabbos: Sabbath
Shacharis: morning service
shaylah: rabbinic consultation
shemesh: sun
shiur: lecture
Shul: synagogue
simchah: joy
Tehillim: Psalms
tof: Hebrew letter